THE LITTLE LONDON NIGHTINGALE

VICTORIAN ROMANCE

JESS WEIR

PUREREAD.COM

CONTENTS

Dear reader, get ready for another great story…	1
Chapter 1	3
Chapter 2	14
Chapter 3	24
Chapter 4	34
Chapter 5	44
Chapter 6	54
Chapter 7	62
Chapter 8	72
Chapter 9	81
Chapter 10	89
Chapter 11	100
Chapter 12	108
Epilogue	115
Other Books By Jess Weir	123
Love Victorian Romance?	125
Our Gift To You	127

DEAR READER, GET READY FOR ANOTHER GREAT STORY...

A VICTORIAN ROMANCE

Turn the page and let's begin

CHAPTER 1

Anna Bailey crept through the hushed crowd. She was small enough to ease her way, weaving back and forth, without causing a fuss. It was easy when Lucy Lawrence was flying through the air; the crowd was too mesmerised to pay much heed to the scruffy girl sneaking her way to the front.

The big top of *Gerrity's Unbelievable Show* was average for a travelling circus of their standard. It was large enough to accommodate seating for those who could afford a few extra coins to sit in comfort, with a pit area for the masses who couldn't. Anna always crept through the pit area. If she tried to wander through the seating, Mr Gerrity might have seen her and lost his famous temper; famous among the performers, at any rate. For anyone paying to see the show, Mr Gerrity was a fine-looking man with a big sense of humour and an even bigger laugh. It seemed that everything, absolutely everything, was a part of the show, even Mr Gerrity's character.

Finally, Anna could see what she had come to see. Lucy, her knees hooking her to the bar of the trapeze, her arms spread wide, flew through the air. The crowd all looked up as one, reminding Anna of the countless times she'd watched migrating birds turning together. She'd always wondered what force drew them to act in unison. Of course, looking at the tipped heads of all those around her, Anna needn't wonder why. Lucy was a true wonder, and as far as Anna was concerned, the star of the show.

"With no safety net, she flies high above the treacherous ground, that earth was ready and waiting to swallow her up!" Mr Gerrity roared, whipping the crowd up into a frenzy.

Anna despised his additions to what should have simply been a thing of beauty. She despised the way he dangled death as a possibility; a possibility the audience lapped up like thirsty dogs.

There was so much to be admired in the performers. Their skill was second to none, defying gravity and even their own bodies to provide a thing of wonder for others to admire. But Anna knew that this wasn't why they were here. Not even the seated ones who had a few extra coins and thought themselves so much better. No, the truth was, they'd all come hoping to see something awful. They were the same sort of people who would have been entertained by public executions.

"One false move and the Flying Fairy will plummet to the earth, smashed to smithereens!" Gerrity bellowed, and the crowd drew in their breath as Lucy, her white-blonde ponytail streaming beneath her like a canary's wing swung higher and higher. All the time, building speed and momentum.

It was an apt description; at just seventeen, Lucy resembled a sweet fairy when her feet were on the ground. In the air, even more so, for her skill in the twists and turns was something of a miracle as she seemed to hover or fly at will.

Holding on with slim, fragile-looking arms, she rolled her body and let go to a gasp of the crowd. Tucking, she twisted in the air as strong and graceful as an eagle on the wing. There was not a sound as she turned and flew an impossible distance to the waiting trapeze that had been swung at just the right moment for her to catch. None of the crowd had noticed it before she grabbed hold and they let out a great sigh of awe.

Lucy's nimble fingers hooked onto the bar, and she unfurled into a beautifully neat, taut straight line as the complicated manoeuvre was completed.

The crowd breathed again, perhaps with a hint of disappointment.

Anna wondered if she were just a little jaded. Could you be jaded at fifteen? She'd been raised in the circus and knew nothing else, and she'd watched crowd after crowd silently willing catastrophe to do its worst. It had, of course, from time to time, and Anna had seen eyes wildly alight with mawkish glee even as the lips proclaimed the awfulness of the whole thing; the tragedy of it. But people loved tragedy. Tragedy was what they were paying to see whether they admitted it to themselves or not.

Of course, there was always tragedy, even if there was not an accident. For the most part, the tragedy displayed daily was the tragedy of birth. The deformed children who had grown up to discover that the only work available was; to make a mockery of themselves and their lives as circus sideshows. For instance, the pinheaded man, his head so small that his body looked horribly wide. Anna felt her heart break every time she looked at him, yet all he ever did was smile. With his brain unable to develop within the constricted walls of so small a skull, he didn't have enough wits to know he was being stared at, mocked, and humiliated. Perhaps that was the only mercy in all of it.

Then there were the women with extraordinary facial and body hair. They seemed to be in constant supply, and she often wondered how it was Mr Gerrity found them. For the most part, the ladies didn't speak a word of English, and she'd never dared to ask where they came from. Circus men always seemed to be able to find the vulnerable; they had a sense for them, a natural talent for drawing them in.

"Our beautiful Flying Fairy lives to fly another day!" Mr Gerrity called out loudly. "But don't forget, we're here all week, ladies and gentlemen. Every day at the circus is different from the day before!" He always grew louder when he tried to tempt them back to spend their coins again.

Anna groaned inwardly. It would have been more honest of him to shout, *"Come back tomorrow, and maybe she really will fall next time!"*

Lucy had flown to the platform high above the crowd, stepping onto it as if it were on the ground. No nerves showed, there was no hint of anything other than the easiest balance. She let go of the trapeze and stood on the tiny platform. She looked beautiful. Her bodysuit was lilac and shone like silk, fine net wings attached to the sleeves, wings which flew when Lucy did. It was an outfit that would only ever be acceptable in the circus, not in the normal day of 1883; not in the England outside of the big top where hems were low and necklines impossibly high. Another one of Mr Gerrity's additions to Lucy's act.

Lucy waved to the crowd; even that simple gesture was filled with balance and grace.

Anna waved back, knowing that Lucy probably couldn't even see her there. She waved because she was grateful;

grateful for a few minutes of escape into a world where it was possible to fly.

"And now, the most amazing trick rider in England, the one and only Bernard Bailey!" Mr Gerrity roared, and the crowd let their attention wander away from the Flying Fairy as she climbed down the rope ladder to safety and prepared themselves for the appearance of Anna's father.

Even as Bernard Bailey flew out into the ring, the clattering of his horse's hooves was loud enough to be heard over the musicians' sudden and wild playing, Anna turned away and eased back through the crowd and out of the big top.

Anna had prepared everything for the evening meal early that day and had only to warm it all through. She had a fire alight outside the high sided carriage that she and her father both lived and travelled in. Setting up a metal tripod, she hung the pan containing the rich stew above the flames.

Anna had already eaten her meal earlier, knowing that her father wouldn't care if she sat down to eat with him or not. The truth was, on the first night in a new town, Anna was always too nervous to eat much as the night went on. Her sense of anxiety simply increased as she cooked and listened to the roar of the crowd inside the big top as they watched the amazing Bernard Bailey charging around the edge of the ring standing on his horse's back. She wondered if they would be so amazed by him if they'd seen how cruelly he treated his horses. If they knew what it took to make performers out of the poor creatures? She shook her head, she knew them, all of them, even though they'd never been introduced. She knew them well enough to know that they wouldn't care one way or the other. People who drew such pleasure from the very sight of the unfortunately born, the prospect of a woman falling to her death, or a beautiful wild animal forced to act against its every instinct, wouldn't care at all about beaten and broken horses.

"I saw you in the crowd today," Lucy said, walking towards her with a bright smile.

"Did you really?" Anna was amazed that a woman who needed every shred of concentration to work the trapeze could spare an ounce of it to look for the star struck girl who admired her so.

"At the end, when I was standing on the platform. I could see you waving at me." Lucy grinned and sat down on the grass beside Anna as she continued to keep an eye on the stew. "Making his dinner then?" she went on.

"Yes, I managed to get a little meat, so he should be happy for that much," Anna said and shrugged. She knew it was unlikely that her father would give her a word of praise about the meal she'd made for him. After all, she didn't get a word of praise for keeping the wooden carriage they lived in clean and orderly, his clothes laundered, his hair cut just the way he liked it, his chin freshly shaved. Surely, it would be easier to look after a baby.

"Are any of them ever happy about anything? I mean…" Lucy had begun conversationally, but her voice trailed away to nothing and Anna followed her gaze. She shouldn't have been surprised to see her father leaning one arm against one of the circus wagons, a young and adoring woman with her back against it looking up at him.

"It's always the same, Lucy. The first night in any town, he always picks up with somebody. I don't know how he does it; look, he's so much older than she is." Anna tried to bite back her disgust.

"Some women like it." Lucy shrugged. "It doesn't matter what he looks like or how old he is, for ten minutes he was the star of the show. I don't understand it myself, but women will throw themselves at any man at all if he was the centre of attention for a while, if all eyes were on him."

"I just wish he'd go somewhere else to… well…" Anna was too embarrassed to finish the sentence. Even though Lucy must surely have realised that Bernard Bailey's conquests were always made in the same little carriage where his daughter was trying to sleep, still, Anna couldn't admit it out loud.

"Why don't you come to me? Look, hand me out your blankets now before he gets here and come over to me as soon as you've finished feeding him. He looks engrossed enough, I'm sure he won't miss you if you sleep in my carriage."

"I'm sure he won't miss me either," Anna said sadly.

"I wish I hadn't said it quite like that, my sweet," Lucy said and put a long, slender arm around Anna's shoulders. "I suppose it's just the life we lead here, isn't it? Never settled anywhere, travelling all the way up the country only to turn around and travel all the way back down again. I suppose, in his own way, your father is lonely."

"I just wish he would go and be lonely in somebody else's carriage," Anna said and shuddered. "It's impossible to sleep when…" Again, she couldn't finish her sentence.

"This is a hard life, no doubt about it. I was born in a circus, Anna, just like you. Only, my father made me train as an acrobat and then a trapeze artist. There was never any choice in it, and he used to pick up women along the way. I understand how you feel," she went on in a soothing voice.

"You're so good at it, Lucy. Don't you like it?"

Lucy's eyes dropped to stare at the ground. There was a desolation about her that Anna had never seen before.

"I hate being here. I hate that I never learned anything else in my life but this." Lucy spread her bird-like arms, and for a moment, Anna thought she would fly away and hover before her like a fairy tale fairy. Of course, she didn't.

"You always look so content on the trapeze."

"It is the only time I *am* content. Being in the middle of the show, Mr Gerrity is not able to bawl and shout and throw things if he doesn't like what he sees. I forget they're all there; Gerrity and his wife, the crowd, everybody. It's the only time I feel free… when I'm flying. But then, like any captive bird, my wings are pushed back down against my body and I'm stuffed back inside the cage." Lucy's beautiful face looked so sad that Anna could have cried; her bright blue eyes, her impossibly pale blonde hair, everything about her so beautiful and for what? So that she could live a life without any choice at all.

"What would you do?" Anna said, her eyes wide looking up at Lucy. "If you were free all the time? If after the show, you weren't pushed back inside a cage?"

The question hung in the air for a few moments, much like Lucy herself would appear to float mid-air, defying gravity, before she would inevitably grab onto the swing and surge forward again.

Lucy looked up at the stars that had started to twinkle in the sky before answering. "I'd go somewhere where beauty isn't bittersweet. Where the audience isn't simply just waiting for you to fall." Lucy looked down at the ground, seemingly picturing the disastrous event in her mind's eye. "Perhaps I'd become a dancer, performing on a big stage, for even bigger audiences. And they would throw me roses and congratulate me on my skill, not for not falling." Lucy's eyes filled with sadness, but a kind smile grew on her face. "But that's all just a dream, so…"

"Dreams are the most important thing we have." Anna said simply. "Dreams are what keep us going, what stops us from simply giving in. Dreams keep us fighting."

Lucy looked over at Anna with a strange expression, one almost of surprise. Such wisdom from such youth.

"Come on then, hand down those blankets, and I'll go and hide them in my carriage. And come to me when you're ready, Anna, don't wait around," Lucy said, forcing herself to speak more brightly and kissing the top of Anna's head.

CHAPTER 2

Anna had to admit that she quite liked Lincoln. Above them, a cathedral and a castle were perched high on a hill. It drew her imagination. What would it be like to be a princess, sitting in that castle and staring down at the common where the travelling circus was setting up? Would it be exciting? Would you have a family, or were those thick sandstone walls just another prison?

She pulled her eyes away and looked around at the folk milling in the streets. She couldn't remember *Gerrity's Unbelievable Show* ever stopping here before, she was sure she would have remembered it. She always had a little time to go out into whatever town they were in and buy provisions for herself and her father, and she had to admit that she liked the look of the place. However, she knew that the people who lined up to get into the big top that evening would be the same as they were anywhere in England. A wave of fatigue washed over her. She seemed to have been travelling up and down the spine of the country her entire life, and she always wondered what it would be like to just live somewhere.

If her mother hadn't died giving birth to her, would they have settled somewhere? Would they have put down roots and lived like normal people? She doubted it; her father had only one skill, and that was trick riding.

Ever since Lucy had allowed her to sleep in her carriage on show nights – which to her shock when she realised, was over a year ago now - Anna had felt a little better about the world she inhabited. She no longer had to listen to her father's noisy activities as each new conquest was made after the show, and it had somehow allowed her emotions to level out, the anxiety lifting bit by bit.

On the second show night in Lincoln, Anna was late going to Lucy's carriage. Her father had insisted that she feed the extraordinarily beautiful young woman who was to be his companion that night. The old man must have been taken with her, for Bernard Bailey didn't ordinarily care whether his companion's belly rumbled or not.

Stirring the pot anxiously, Anna had been forced to make a little food go a lot further. It was possible by cutting the bread a little thinner and buttering it, adding little slices of the cheese that she had hoped would last them for the rest of the week. The young woman tried to smile at her, but Anna focused on what she was doing, unable to make eye contact. This was just another in a long line of young women whose quest for a little excitement had often made Anna's life all the harder. Her heart told her she should be kind, even try and warn the young lady, but she couldn't bring herself to even look at her. It was easier that way, keeping out of the way.

By the time she reached Lucy's carriage, it was almost midnight. Not late for circus people, it was true, for there was still much clearing away going on and even one or two of the audience still milling about.

"Lucy? Lucy, are you awake?" Anna asked in a whisper as she climbed up the wooden steps and into the back of the carriage.

It was as black as night inside, but Anna could hear heavy breathing and muffled sniffling. Was that Lucy? Was she crying?

"Lucy?" Anna said, blindly searching for a match in the darkness so that she might light the oil lamp.

"Anna? Oh, Anna," Lucy said, and her voice was thick with emotion, even fear, Anna thought. She hurriedly got the lamp alight, put the glass shade over it, and turned to look for Lucy.

Lucy was curled in a ball on her bed, her knees drawn into her chest, her arms wrapped around her shins. Anna squinted in the gloom and realised that Lucy had a dark bruise on her cheek.

"What happened?" she asked, but Lucy shook her head and buried herself back in the protection of her arms. "Are you all right? What happened?"

Lucy looked up, and even though she looked at Anna, she seemed to be looking right through her, and it frightened Anna.

"You'd better try and get some sleep," Lucy said, her voice far off, as if in a dream. She seemed to be in a trance and Anna could see that she was rocking very slightly from side to side as she lay on her bed.

"Lucy, who did this to you?"

"Mr Gerrity," Lucy said in an exhausted voice. "Mr Gerrity did this, but you can't tell anybody. If you tell anybody, I'll be thrown out of here, thrown out onto the streets. And as Mr Gerrity said, I won't survive on the streets. I need him, don't I? No matter what he does to me, I still need him."

"Lucy, what are you talking about?" Anna asked, her heart breaking for her one true friend. Need Mr Gerrity? Why would Lucy be talking like this?

"I told him that I wanted to leave, that I wanted to move on, and he—" Lucy's voice caught in her throat. She swallowed, coughed, and then continued. "He became so nasty, I think he was already in a temper. It was silly of me to mention it now, but after that last show I just couldn't take it anymore."

"He hit you?" Anna's voice quivered.

"Yes." Lucy said flatly. "He said that people like me don't get dreams. That we were put on this earth to fuel the dreams of others... I was born to fuel his dream. He told me that if I even mentioned leaving again, he would publicly shame me, make sure no one would want or take me. Then he said he would..." Lucy's eyes glanced over at Anna, and the tears started anew. "Oh Anna, dreams are the most ghastly things. They give us hope when there isn't any." Lucy took another ragged breath. "After the first hit, he didn't believe I'd learnt my lesson, so he hit me again and again." She traced her swelling face with her finger. She wistfully added, "Made sure it wasn't bad enough that it couldn't be covered up though, always thinking of the show."

"Lucy, I should have been here. My father made me cook for his latest woman, it kept me back. Oh, may God forgive me! If I'd been here..."

"If you'd been here, he wouldn't have cared. I'm so glad you weren't here. I'm so glad you weren't here to see and to suffer."

"But you had to suffer alone," Anna said, tears running down her face even as Lucy's own tears had dried and the pale face of shock had set in.

Anna lifted the small chipped porcelain jug which Lucy kept in the corner of the carriage, tipping some water into a bowl and soaking a cloth. She wrung it out and tenderly dabbed the cool cloth against the violent bruise on Lucy's face.

"Come on, Lucy, let's get you cleaned up."

The following night, Anna was amazed that there was no sign of bruising on Lucy's beautiful face. She was high up in the air, of course, but she must have used a good deal of greasepaint to hide the evil blemish.

Anna had squeezed her way through the crowd, as she always did, and hoped that Lucy would know she was there in amongst them, silently supporting her as always, loving her dearly. Anna hadn't been able to sleep a wink the previous night and she still felt shocked and sick when she thought of what Lucy had suffered. She'd been unable to look at Mr Gerrity whenever she'd passed him that day, for now that she knew what a filthy, evil man he was, she was certain that he would see the disgust in her eyes.

"One false move and the Flying Fairy will plummet to the earth, smashed to smithereens!" Mr Gerrity bellowed; it was the same thing night after night after night.

They had reached the part of the performance where Lucy ordinarily rolled her slim body through her arms as she held tightly to the trapeze bar. However, the trapeze was slowly swinging this way and that as Lucy hung beneath it straight and still. She was staring ahead of her, seeming somehow not to realise where she was, and Anna's heart began to pound.

"One false move and the Flying Fairy will plummet to the earth, smashed to smithereens!" Mr Gerrity said again, bellowing even louder this time as if to break through Lucy's little trance and have her remember where she was and exactly what she ought to be doing at that moment. However, it didn't break through.

To Anna's horror, Lucy turned her head. The trapeze had slowed to a standstill now, Lucy's arms lean and strong, and her fingers clasping the bar. She seemed to be looking for somebody, and when her head had stopped moving, Anna realised that she was looking for her. Lucy held her rooted to the spot with her determined gaze and Anna saw her nod; a gentle and almost imperceptible nod. She mouthed the words "I'm sorry". And then, she just let go. She opened her hands, her fingers splayed, and she plummeted to the earth, to be smashed to smithereens just as Mr Gerrity declared she might.

Anna cried out, her scream barely audible over the sudden yells of excitement which rippled through the crowd. There was a great surge as everybody pushed forward, the people at the back so keen to be close to the scene of carnage at the front. Anna was carried along with the crowd, pushed against the wooden barrier at the front, which held them all back from the ring.

She was hemmed in tight, her chest squeezed between the wood of the barrier and the weight of the people behind her. Anna was trapped where she was, confronted with the sight of Lucy's still moving body on the floor of the ring, unable to escape, unable to climb over and get to her, to spend those last minutes of Lucy's life holding her hand.

Lucy had landed with her head turned away, and Anna wished she could at least have seen her there, to have known that her friend was reaching for her, caring for her. Finally, the tiny movements which seemed to make Lucy twitch, ceased and Anna knew that the life had gone out of her body at last.

Mr Gerrity was shouting, calling out for blankets to be brought to cover Lucy as she lay dead for all to see. He was trying to get the crowd to move back, calling out to the performers to help free those trapped against the barrier at the front. It was absolute mayhem, pandemonium, and yet Anna didn't care if she was crushed to death.

At just fifteen years old, Anna felt as if she had now lost everything. Lucy was the only person in the world who cared about her, who had given her a moment's consideration. Lucy had inspired her, made her see the beauty in life every time she looked up and saw her gracefully flying through the air, her incredible physical strength hidden inside her narrow frame, her graceful limbs.

Anna knew that Lucy couldn't have stood to have lived out the rest of her life with the fulfilling of the dreams of the awful cruelty of Mr Gerrity. He had crushed all the hoping and dreaming out of her, until she had eventually snapped, and he had crushed the will to live out of her too. Without even knowing it – or maybe he did and just didn't care – he'd snatched away Lucy Lawrence's hopes for a future somewhere else, somewhere far, far away from the big top and the circus.

It was such a terrible waste. A beautiful life destroyed. What a cruel, foul world this was! At that point, Anna stopped struggling. Her tired arms, which had been braced against the wooden barrier in an attempt to stop her from being crushed, simply gave up, and went limp. If Lucy was gone, what was the point in Anna still being here? This was her opportunity to let go, just as Lucy had. Lucy had let go of the trapeze bar, and Anna had taken her hands away from the wooden barrier; in the end, wasn't it the same thing? Wasn't it all just giving up on a life that didn't seem to be worth living?

What did it matter that she was only fifteen years old? Lucy Lawrence had only been seventeen and nobody would miss her either, nobody but Anna. It was time to go, it was time to join Lucy in a place that was better than this.

As she felt her lungs constricted, hot and unable to draw breath, Anna, closed her eyes and let go. The world turned black, and she waited for the nightmare to end. Sliding into unconsciousness, she didn't feel the large hands of her father hook under her armpits and drag her roughly over the top of the barrier and into the circus ring.

CHAPTER 3

It was some months later, and Anna still couldn't think about Lucy without tears stinging her eyes. Lucy had been a light in her darkness, and she missed that light every single day. Anna hated Mr Gerrity with what she could only describe as a deep passion. She despised the very ground he laid his feet on, the air he breathed, and she no longer felt any pity for his lumpen wife, Margaret.

Anna had it in her head that Mrs Gerrity had known exactly what her husband had done to young Lucy. Yet still, she stood by his side, bullying the performers to please him, scowling at any of the prettier and younger young women who travelled with the circus. How could she lay down every night at the side of a man who could do something so terrible? Anna knew that she herself could not be married to such a man, no matter the consequences of leaving him.

Hearing the same tired old strains of music which heralded the end of her father's performance for the night, the thrilled and excited applause which was bestowed upon him, Anna hung the pot of stew above the fire. It wouldn't be long before he appeared unless he'd settled upon a companion for the night who might need a little more convincing than the rest. Still, even that wouldn't take him long.

Anna was amazed by his success, given that there was absolutely nothing whatsoever about him which could be described as handsome, nor even really pleasant. If only she had a father she could love, a father whom she could admire and look up to. Not this base creature who seemed to be nothing more than a great long list of needs. He needed to be fed, to be kept clean, to be attended to by one of the local women whenever he required. Apart from riding his horse around the ring at breakneck speed, Bernard Bailey added nothing to the world, he only ever took. Anna scolded herself for such thinking, knowing it wasn't very virtuous, but it was becoming more and more difficult to be kind and caring, when no one seemed to be kind and caring towards her. Lucy was the only one, and now she was gone.

Anna looked up to see him walking towards her, hand in hand with a young woman whose delighted giggle she could hear from two hundred yards away. Well, this one didn't take much convincing, she supposed. What amazed Anna was the sheer number of young women who willingly threw themselves onto the path of a man like her father. Surely, they knew it was fleeting; perhaps that was the attraction, who knew?

"There will be enough for two, won't there?" her father said, making his demand seem like a question for the benefit of the young woman on his arm.

"Yes, Father," Anna said and climbed up into the carriage to retrieve another tin bowl. She jumped down, setting out the two bowls on the ground and ladling in the hot vegetable stew. As her father sat down on the blanket by the fire with his companion, Anna handed them the bowls and spoons, pushing forward a basket of roughly cut bread.

The young woman looked thrilled; perhaps she didn't see this as rough and impoverished but rather as exciting and romantic. Well, let *her* be the one to live this way then and see how romantic the silly creature thought it then.

Anna had already rolled her heaviest blanket into a little cotton bag she had made for herself. She reached into the carriage to retrieve it from where she had left it close to the door. Tucking it under her arm, she wandered away unseen into the night. Her father was already too besotted to notice or care, never once asking her where she spent the nights when he was not alone.

She sadly walked past the carriage which had once belonged to Lucy. Her heart lurched; it was the setting of so much joy and laughter between the two friends, not to mention the setting for so much horror for poor Lucy. It stood as a monument to a crushed dream for Anna. Anna paused for a moment. She realised she didn't have a dream of her own. She didn't know a world outside of the circus and her father's infidelities. She had no clue where she would want to go if she was ever set free. Maybe it was better that way, as Lucy had said. Dreams give hope that can only be crushed. Anna gave one last glance at the carriage before starting to walk again.

It was now inhabited by another trapeze artist, a strong and sinewy young Eastern European woman called Ingrid. Ingrid was beautiful in her own way, but nowhere near as beautiful as Lucy had been. She paid no heed to Anna at all, the two of them spoke different languages, and Ingrid seemed to have no interest in the girl who so often walked by her carriage.

Ingrid was pretty enough to worry about, had it not been for the fact that she was part of a double act, her husband also being a trapeze artist. No doubt that had irritated Mr Gerrity, the idea that he was not the all-powerful male presence in her life. However, trapeze artists were hard to find, and it cheered her a little to think that he'd had to take what he could get, even if it included a husband.

Anna spent an hour sitting in a field in the darkness, waiting for the big top to finally be cleared of not only the audience but of all the performers who had to set everything straight before they went to bed. They didn't all go to bed immediately, of course, for they were night people for the most part. She could hear talking and laughing, voices which seemed to grow ever drunker, and she let the sounds wash over her before making her way into the big top.

She went to the very back, behind the great curtain which separated the circus ring from what might have been described as *backstage*. It was deserted, and so she wrapped her blanket around herself and curled up on a hard wooden bench for the night. She would be cold and uncomfortable, but at least she would be able to sleep without the nauseating sound of… Anna shuddered at the thought.

She fell asleep with surprising speed, waking an hour or two later when she heard voices a little too close to the canvas walls of the big top for comfort. Rising to a sitting position, her blanket still around her shoulders, Anna strained to listen. Surely, that was her father's voice she could hear, but who was he talking to? Perhaps he was saying good night to his companion, dismissing her before the day had even broken. What a prince he was!

"No, I've never been to America before," her father said, his voice all politeness and curiously refined. It made her listen all the harder.

"You're gonna love it, Mr Bailey!" said a rather enthusiastic voice, a male voice speaking with an

American accent. Who on earth was it? Why did her father need to speak to somebody in the middle of the night?

"Well, you've seen my skill for yourself, so I reckon it's up to you to decide now, Mr Marston," her father said, still polite and refined, but his arrogance beginning to shine through as it always did in the end.

"I sure did, I sure did," Mr Marston said, clearly unperturbed by the arrogance of Bernard Bailey. "So, we set sail from Southampton. You'll be there, will you not? You'll square it all with Mr Gerrity and come work for me in America? You won't be sorry you did. The pay is good, and the crowds are huge. The circus sure is big business over there."

"It's all I've ever wanted, Mr Marston," her father said, and Anna's eyes widened; were they going to America? Were they going to be leaving Mr Gerrity and his lumpen wife for good? "I can promise you I won't be missing an opportunity like this."

"And you've no wife? No family? My travelling circus travels light, no room for any extras, if you know what I mean. But you needn't worry, you'll still be able to pick yourself up a companion or two along the way." The man laughed in a way which sickened Anna; *were they all the same?* "Just so long as you remember to set them back down again where you picked them up. No hangers-on, you understand?"

"No, hangers-on! And no, I've no wife. I've no family at all," Bernard said, and Anna's mouth dropped open. *No family at all?* But he had a daughter! Surely, he wasn't going to leave the country without her!

"Well, that's all settled then. Take this, I've written everything down, the times of sailings and whatnot. I'll expect to see you." Mr Marston's voice was trailing off, and she knew that he was walking away.

She got up and crept to the other side of the big top, straining to listen.

"Now then, I'll get out of here before anyone sees me. I know what a temper that ringmaster of yours has!" he went on, laughing.

Anna couldn't hear her father's response; the two men were now too far away for that. She felt powerless standing there, wanting to chase after her father and ask him if it was true, but knowing that she would earn herself a good hard slap across the face for having eavesdropped in the first place. Why was it never possible to win? And what was going to happen to her now? More than ever, she wished that Lucy had stayed with her.

"You can't go without me, Father, you just can't!" Anna said almost a week later. Her father had said nothing of the fact that he was leaving her until he had begun to pack his suitcase. That was how much he thought of her, that she didn't even deserve the consideration of a little more notice.

"I'll be coming back for you, you silly girl," he said without any hint of conviction. "You just stay here with Mr Gerrity and wait for me."

"But I don't work for Mr Gerrity, Father. I've never been employed by Mr Gerrity, I'm just here with you. Without your money, how am I to eat? How am I to survive?"

"Well, you'll be working for Mr Gerrity now." He shrugged and turned away from her to continue with his packing.

"Doing what? You've never trained me for any of the acts in the circus!"

"You never had any talent for it, I could see that just by looking at you," her father snapped; he'd had enough of her complaints now and had become suddenly cruel, as he always did when a conversation became awkward.

"But what am I to do? What is my job to be?" She began to feel terrified.

"You'll be keeping things clean, costumes and what have you. You'll be doing a little cooking, nothing you haven't done before. Stop your whining, girl, you're starting to get on my nerves."

"But whose costumes? And who will I be cooking for?"

"As many as Mr Gerrity tells you to cook for. Whatever he tells you to do, you just do it. In return, he will feed you, clothe you, and allow you to stay in our little carriage. So, you're not going to starve to death, are you?"

"So, I'm not to be paid for my work, then?" she said, unable to stop her voice from dripping with disgust. She wasn't going to be working for Mr Gerrity, her father had simply given her to him. For no pay, Anna was to work her guts out from morning till night, she had no doubt about that. It was survival and nothing more. Mr Gerrity was just going to be taking her father's place, expecting her to work her fingers to the bone for nothing more than a wooden roof over her head and a bellyful of vegetable stew.

"I'm getting tired of this, girl. I'm your father, and I tell you how things are going to be, not the other way around. Now, you work hard for Mr Gerrity, or else he might cast you out of here. Now, he said that you can work for him, but if you don't pull your weight, I'm sure he won't see any need to keep you around."

"Then how would you find me when you come back from America?"

"Oh, I'm too busy to think about nonsense like that now, child," he said in a dismissive tone.

"When are you coming back?" she went on, pushing.

"It depends," he said the evasively.

"What does it depend on?"

"Oh, just get out of here! I'm trying to concentrate on this, and you're distracting me. If I hear another peep out of you, you'll be sorry for it, believe me!" he said, shouting now, ignoring the tears of his only child.

CHAPTER 4

In the months since her father had left for America, Anna had become no better than a skivvy for the entire circus. There were few who showed her much kindness, treating her as if she were an idiot much of the time.

"You haven't cleaned my outfit properly, girl," Ingrid snapped at her one day as she passed the carriage that used to be Lucy's. "You will have to clean it again. You don't work hard enough; I don't know why Mr Gerrity keeps you here! You don't even have any talent, you're not even a performer. You're nothing!" she went on cruelly in her rich Eastern European accent.

Ingrid had quickly mastered the English language enough to be able to berate Anna whenever she felt like it. Fortunately, her husband held his tongue, but likely Ingrid had enough venom for both of them. He did sometimes smile apologetically at Anna after some of Ingrid's most scathing remarks.

"It's perfectly clean, Ingrid," Anna huffed back, heading to the animal cages with a bucket full of meat to feed the two tigers. The bucket was almost the size of her head, and the smell of the flesh made Anna's head spin; she still hadn't gotten used to it.

"It is not, you will do it again," Ingrid said and marched across to Anna, pushing her hard. Anna lost her balance a little and let go of the bucket, the freshly cut meat spilling out all over the ground.

"Just leave it in my carriage, Ingrid," Anna said, holding onto her anger; she couldn't push back against this woman, she knew she didn't stand a chance against somebody who was strong enough to support their weight with one hand as they flew through the air so high up in the big top.

Anna crouched down and began to pick the raw meat off the ground and put it back into the bucket. Even if it was covered in mud, the tigers would still eat it. At least *they* would be grateful. She sighed, feeling tears in her eyes when she heard a low chuckle. Somebody was laughing at her, enjoying her plight, and she looked up to see the pinheaded man staring at her.

His face looked vacant; his head so small that Anna could barely look at him. She felt so sorry for him, she always had. He extended one hand out to Anna, offering to help her up. She graciously took it.

"Sorry, my hands are all muddy and sticky from the uh…" Anna motioned down at the tiger's spilt meal.

The pinheaded man just shrugged. His face contorted into what Anna had learnt was his way of smiling. She smiled back. Even though his life had surely been unrelenting cruelty, he never let anyone truly crush him. He kept smiling – well, his version of smiling – and sauntering about his day with the slight swagger his gait had. He nodded, and wandered off again, his arms swinging by his side. Anna finished picking up all the meat, and headed to the large tent which housed the animal cages.

The beautiful pair of tigers paced back and forth in cages just large enough for them to turn in. Using the metal spike, just as Mr Gerrity had taught her, she skewered each piece of thick red meat in her bucket and gently eased it through the bars. The tigers snatched at the meat, something which had terrified her months ago when her father had just left, when this had first become one of her many duties. Now, however, she was immune to it. Anna was more affected by the tigers' caged state, the fact that they seemed to have no power in the world. And wasn't she just the same?

How she missed Lucy. How Lucy would have cared for her and helped her through all of this. The feeling of despair came over her for she knew she had nothing. No hope, no life, all that was lost when Lucy died, when she too was lost to the world.

As was always the case when she thought of her friend, Anna's eyes filled with tears. Alone, as the tigers ate the large meal which would subdue them for the night's performance, Anna began to sing. It was a sad song; a popular song she had no memory of consciously learning, but she knew it all the same.

She turned the bucket on its end and sat on it, enjoying the solitude of the animal tent as she sang her broken heart out.

"Tears, idle tears, I know not what they mean,

Tears from the depth of some divine despair

Rise in the heart, and gather to the eyes,

In looking on the happy Autumn fields,

And thinking of the days that are no more."

Anna drew a breath, ready to sing it again when she was aware that she was no longer alone. She looked up and saw a man standing a few feet from her, a fine-looking man in the clothes of a gentleman. With a gasp, she rose from her perch on the upturned bucket and looked at him with fear.

"Forgive me, miss, but I heard your beautiful singing and found myself wandering your way." He smiled and bowed his apology at her.

"This is the animal enclosure, sir." She felt confused, she had never been confronted by anybody there before. "Does Mr Gerrity know that you're here? Should I fetch him for you?"

"Goodness me, no," the man said and began to laugh. "I don't expect he'd be at all pleased to find a stranger wandering about before the show has even started."

"Then you've come to see the show, sir?"

"Yes, I have. I suppose I'm a little early, but I'm very glad to be. I have heard that song sung many times, my dear, but never with such feeling."

"I thought I was alone, sir," she said, feeling embarrassed.

He really did have a nice face. He was older than her, but still a young one. He was perhaps twenty-one or two, with dark brown hair and pale blue eyes. He wore a fine suit in black, a grey overcoat on top of it. His collars were high and stiff, his tie black and pristine. He wore no hat, and she was glad; a top hat would have made such a handsome young man look older, more serious. Instead, he looked friendly and kind.

"Tell me, do you sing as part of the show? Perhaps you are an interval singer?"

"We don't have a singer during the interval, sir. Mr Gerrity says there's no real point to it," she said, her mind working ten to the dozen as she wondered who this fine young man was.

"What a pity, I have a feeling that you would have been the high point of the evening," he smiled at her, and she smiled back; was he mocking her, or did he truly mean it?

"What part do you play in the show then, if you do not sing?"

"I don't play any part in the show, sir. I just work for the performers. I clean and cook and feed the animals, nothing more than that."

"But why?"

"Because I don't have any talent, sir," she said, remembering not only her father's words of months ago but Ingrid's when she had pushed her and made such a fool of her. The man looked aghast; his eyes were wide, and his eyebrows were raised.

"Nobody hearing you sing could imagine that you have no talent, my dear. God has given you the most beautiful, heartfelt singing voice I've ever heard. You are a Nightingale, a real Nightingale." He smiled at her, and Anna felt so emotional that she was afraid she might cry; nobody had paid her so much kind attention since Lucy had died.

"And what in the world is going on in here?" It was clear from the way he burst in through the flap in the canvas that Mr Gerrity had been standing outside for some time. If he hadn't, she might have heard him approaching.

Anna was mute, fearing a beating or worse. The young man, on the other hand, smiled at Mr Gerrity and held his hands up, palms forward, as if in surrender.

"Forgive me, sir, I'm a little early, and I suppose I have been wandering where I ought not to be," the man said, no hint of nerves or fear in his voice.

"Tell me another one, and I won't believe that neither!" Mr Gerrity said in a rough voice. "You London music hall types are always scouting about looking to steal talent from me, and I won't have it, do you hear me? Now, get out of here and be gone from this place. If I set eyes on you again tonight, I'll gut you and feed you to the tigers, and that's the truth!" Mr Gerrity said, and none hearing him would have doubted his sincerity.

The mystery young man turned back to Anna. "You'll be in my prayers, Nightingale." He smiled, and then turned and walked away with a final defiant look at Mr Gerrity.

∽

Anna had fallen asleep early that night, as she did so often these days. Her exhaustion after so much hard physical labour usually meant that her eyes closed the moment her head hit the pillow. However, she hadn't been asleep for long before she was awoken by movement in the carriage. She became sharp in a heartbeat, sitting bolt upright in her bed, her hands scrabbling for the matches on the table beside her.

"You shouldn't have spoken to that man, girl!" It was Mr Gerrity's voice; the man who had beaten Lucy was now in her carriage in the dead of night. Her hands were shaking violently, and she dropped the matches without managing to light one. She blinked rapidly, willing her eyes to focus, to search for the door, to find a way out.

"He just came into the tent, Mr Gerrity, when I was feeding the animals. I didn't invite him, he just appeared," Anna said and could hear her voice trembling.

"I won't have talent scouts coming here and stealing from me, do you hear me?"

"But I don't have any talent, Mr Gerrity. I've never been trained for anything. Why would any talent scout come looking for me? He was just wandering around, I promise. It wasn't my fault, he just appeared." Anna became more and more afraid when she heard his breathing become laboured. She could smell liquor in the air, strong liquor, and she realised that Mr Gerrity was drunk.

"Now then, I wouldn't say you don't have any talent at all, Anna," he said, his voice suddenly low and his tone something which he likely thought to be soothing. To Anna, however, it was a horrible and sinister indication of what was to come next. "That brown hair of yours, those big brown eyes, I wouldn't say you have no talent. And you're not a child anymore, are you? What are you now? Nineteen?"

"No, I'm seventeen. I have only just turned seventeen, Mr Gerrity," she said, utterly panic-stricken, every nerve standing to attention, her mind filled with the awful sight of Lucy curled into a ball on her bed, her cheeks swollen and bruised.

"Seventeen eh? That be the age when girls start thinking they're women." Mr Gerrity took a lumbering step towards her. "And start thinking they can think for themselves."

She began to back away, her eyes slowly adjusting to the gloom. She could see the moonlight on the other side of the partially open carriage door, only she knew her path to that moonlight was blocked now. Tears of fear streamed down her face, and she sniffed loudly.

"There's no need for tears now, is there? I'm not going to hurt you, am I?" There was a dark threat in his voice. "As long as you behave, and stay here. What did that man call you? A nightingale. Yes… You are a nightingale. *My* nightingale. You understand me? You are to always be my side, and you will never ever leave."

"You hurt Lucy! You hurt her so badly that she let herself fall from the trapeze that night. She couldn't bear it, Mr Gerrity, she couldn't bear what you'd done to her. How you'd trapped her here by killing her dreams!" As she spoke, Mr Gerrity became as still as a statue. Perhaps her words were getting through; perhaps he had known all along that he was to blame for a young woman of just seventeen letting go of her grip on life. "You really did hurt her, and she killed herself because of it. So, you mustn't, Mr Gerrity, you mustn't do it again," she said, her voice pleading as if for her very life.

Suddenly, he reached out and gripped her by the hair, pulling her so sharply down to the floor. He raised a hand to slap her across the face. She hadn't made him see sense; she had angered him. She had confronted him with the consequence of his crime, the truth that he had Lucy's blood on his hands, and this was him fighting against that truth.

At the moment that she knew she couldn't escape, that Mr Gerrity was going to do the same to her as he had to Lucy, she drew in a great breath and screamed louder than she had ever screamed in her life.

CHAPTER 5

Even though Mr Gerrity had clapped a hand firmly over her mouth, still her scream had been heard throughout the silence of the circus at night. She could hear footsteps and mumbling outside before the door to the carriage was opened and the room flooded with moonlight. Mr Gerrity turned, grumbling angrily, his hand sliding away from her face.

"Help me, please help me! He's trying to hurt me! Please, please help me!" she yelled, her voice full of fear.

"Gerrity!" The voice was unmistakable; it was the deep and dull tone of Mrs Margaret Gerrity. It was enough to have her husband scamper off the floor and get to his feet, weaving drunkenly as he tried to keep his balance.

"You know what these girls are like, my sweet. You know how they are always trying to buck against the rules, Margaret," Mr Gerrity said in a matter-of-fact tone which made Anna furious. "Found this one sugaring up to a talent scout, and packing her bags to be off and deserting us."

"I was asleep when he came in, Mrs Gerrity. You must believe me!" Anna pulled her blankets around her, using them as a shield as she stood to her feet.

"You ought to be ashamed of yourself, girl," Margaret Gerrity said, although Anna could tell from the note of betrayal in her voice that she didn't really believe it for a minute. She knew what her husband was. However, she wasn't about to admit it to herself. No doubt it would serve Margaret Gerrity's heart a little better to have somebody else to blame.

"Mrs Gerrity, please!"

Mrs Gerrity took an excruciatingly long time to respond. Her eyes flicked from Anna up to her husband, and back down to Anna. She took in a sharp breathe, seemingly having made a decision.

"I can't have her here, Kelvin. I can't have immoral girls like that travelling with us. No, she has to go!" Mrs Gerrity's tone had become determined now. "Now!"

"Gone, my dear?" An underlying panic suddenly appeared in Mr Gerrity's voice. "But that's exactly what she wants! We can't have her—"

"I will not have rats in my ship, you understand me Kelvin?" Mrs Gerrity's voice held an authority. "If she was going to desert us, we might as well throw her out ourselves. Right away, so she can't organise to be picked up by the talent scout. We will leave her alone. The streets will soon teach her the lessons she needs."

Mr Gerrity struggled for words. His own lies had gotten him into this situation. And perhaps Mrs Gerrity was slightly more perceptive, and more kind, than Anna had first given her credit for.

Mr Gerrity was quickly expelled from the carriage as Mrs Gerrity stood over Anna while she both dressed and then packed her few belongings. Anna was going to be thrown out into the night, she was going to be dumped in the city of London without friends, family, nor even a penny to her name, but at least she would be free. Margaret Gerrity couldn't give Anna much, but she was giving the young girl something Lucy had never had the chance to have: freedom.

∼

Terrified, Anna walked through the park, away from the circus, praying as she went that the moon would not disappear behind a cloud again. When it did, it was so terribly dark she felt as if she had been struck blind.

At first, Anna had thought to sleep in the park, to wrap a blanket around her and lean against one of the many trees. However, she heard voices now and again, drunken male voices. Perhaps it would be safer to make her way out of the park and into the streets.

They'd been to London many times, the entourage of *Gerrity's Unbelievable Show*, enough for her to know that it was vast. All she knew of her current surroundings was that the circus had set up in Vauxhall Park, and she could only assume that she was now in the area of Vauxhall as she made her way onto the streets. She kept walking and could see the River Thames shining black in the distance, and so she headed for it. Perhaps there would be somewhere for her to sleep for a while, or somebody there she could ask for help. But who would help her? Why would anybody help her now? She knew that London was teeming with poor people, those who lived and died on the streets. Was she now to become one of them?

She could see by the light of the moon there were many benches along the embankment of the River Thames. However, she could also see that many of them were already inhabited by rough men who had thought to get a few hours' sleep there, just as she had. So, Anna turned away from the river and began to walk east. She'd walked for almost an hour before she found a seemingly deserted street. There were large terraced houses, so tall and so wide that she knew there could only be fine families living here. There was a square, a widening of the road that was fenced off and contained the tiniest little park she'd ever seen. It was a small square with very little cover, but there was a bench there, and so she finally sat down on it.

Exhausted right down to her very bones, Anna closed her eyes and, unbelievably, she slept.

∼

"Oi, what you doing here? Nobody ever sleeps here on this bench, the folks in Cleaver Square don't hold with that sort of thing." Hearing the childish voice, Anna's eyelids began to flutter until her eyes were open and she found herself staring at a little boy of perhaps eight or nine years.

He had a rough London accent, but his clothes were not quite as impoverished as so many other little boys of his age. He looked reasonably clean too, and she looked at him with interest as her mind began to awaken, and she remembered the horror of the night before and the desperation of her new situation.

"Cleaver Square?" she said, confused.

"Yes, Cleaver Square! That's where you are now, miss, didn't you know?"

"No, I didn't know," she said and wanted to cry.

"This is Cleaver Square in Kennington. It's in London, you know," he went on. The little boy looked over his shoulder for a moment before sitting down on the bench next to her.

"Yes, I know I'm in London. I was with the circus; I was in Vauxhall Park."

"The circus!" The little boy said, his eyes growing round with excitement. "I would give anything to be in the circus! I would give anything to just see it!" He shrugged then and became conspiratorial. "Well, I have seen it once, miss. Don't tell anybody, but a couple of nights ago, I snuck in under the canvas." He grinned at her.

"Don't worry, I won't tell anybody," Anna said vacantly, her mind hardly on the conversation at all.

"But what are you doing here, miss? Why were you sleeping on the bench?" It was barely light, and she wondered why he was out so early in the morning.

"Because I was thrown out of the circus, thrown out in the middle of the night. Now I have nowhere to go, and no money and I don't know what to do," she said, tears rolling down her face, hardly able to believe that she was sharing her cares with a child.

"Why?"

"You're too young to understand it, and you wouldn't be any better off knowing it anyway."

"What are you going to do now?"

"I don't know. I've only ever lived with the circus folk. I don't know how to live outside of that world."

"Were you a lion tamer?"

"No, I was just the girl who cleaned up everybody's mess, washed their clothes, and cooked their meals. No talent," she said, suddenly thinking of the kind young man whose innocent words had somehow brought her here. He had said she would be in his prayers. Well, if he was praying for her to get away from Mr Gerrity, God had answered, but how fortunate of a thing that would be remained to be seen.

"If you can clean up messes and cook and what have you, I think you're going to be all right," the little boy said, smiling brightly at her, seeming pleased as if he'd solved all her problems in the blink of an eye.

"Do you think so?" she asked sadly, not wanting to explain to the boy that there was nothing that could be done for her, not when he was clearly trying so hard.

"I know it. I can help you, but I can see you don't believe me. You think I'm too little to help, don't you?" He looked mildly affronted and she couldn't help but smile at him.

"I'm sorry, I suppose I've just had a very difficult night."

"I know where you can get a job." He quickly got over his hurt feelings and looked triumphant.

"Do you really?" Anna hardly dared let her heart hope.

"Yes, with Mr and Mrs Leyland. They live right over there," he said and pointed clear across the square to one of the large, fine terraced houses. "Mrs Bunker has just had to let the scullery maid go. Well, she didn't *have* to let 'er go, she dismissed 'er. Mrs Bunker is allowed to do that, you see… because she's the housekeeper."

"Why did she dismiss the scullery maid?" Anna asked, feeling some solidarity for the unknown young female.

"I don't know, but she was really cross!" the little boy said and shrugged. "But she's still cross because she needs somebody to help below stairs. If you tell her that you know how to help with the cooking and washing sheets and sweeping up and cleaning boots and anything else like that, she might just take you. You speak nicely too, not like we do around here. Where are you from?"

"Everywhere and nowhere," Anna said, hardly seeing the little boy's look of confusion. It was true, she had no discernible accent, no roots, and none of the culture that growing up in one place provides.

"You look nice and clean too; Mrs Bunker likes that sort of thing. She wouldn't take you on if you looked like you been sleeping on the streets. I know you're not supposed to tell lies, but maybe you should. Maybe you should say that you decided to leave the circus, not that they threw you out. She's a suspicious sort, Mrs Bunker. The truth is, she's not very nice at all, but what housekeeper is?"

"Do you work in that house?"

"Yes, I have done since I was six, and I'm eight now. It was that or the workhouse, so I made my decision hasty like." He grinned at her, suddenly seeming much older than his years. "I help with the horses mostly, but I'm at Mrs Bunker's beck and call too. She's made me set off early this morning to collect bread from the baker. His lad's gone sick, you see, so he won't be able to deliver this morning. She wants me back in time for making Mr and Mrs Leyland's breakfast."

"Perhaps you'd better go. You don't want to get into trouble with Mrs Bunker, do you?" she said gently, feeling some affection for the little boy who seemed so determined to help her.

"And you'll go over to the house and ask for some work? Look, you go down the side there, between the two big houses, and there's a little brown door right at the back. You have to go down some stairs to it, but you'll find Mrs Bunker there. See that you knock on the door first, though, because that's just something else she doesn't like!" he said and chuckled.

"Then I'll do just that," Anna said and got to her feet, straightening her dress and pressing down her thick brown hair. "What's your name?" she asked as the little boy got ready to take his leave.

"Billy. My name is Billy," he said and suddenly thrust his hand out like a little gentleman.

"Well, I'm Anna. It's nice to meet you, Billy. I hope we'll be working together," she said, taking his little hand and holding it firmly as her eyes wandered over to the large terraced house.

CHAPTER 6

"And you can get that lot out to dry before you start clearing away the breakfast plates. Come on, girl, this isn't the circus. You have to work hard here for your money," Mrs Bunker said disdainfully.

After six months of solid hard work, still, the housekeeper made a point of berating Anna whenever she had the opportunity. She was a curious woman, having taken Anna on after the very briefest interview, seemingly impressed by the fact that the girl was clean and tidy, experienced in the art of taking care of a great many people, and could read and write. However, Mrs Bunker disliked the circus. She'd never been, of course, but she'd heard tell from many who had and she didn't hold with that sort of thing, she didn't hold with it at all.

As far as Mrs Bunker was concerned, circus performers were to be scorned, never pitied. Those who had deformities had been blighted by God for previous sins, and the rest were simply immoral, lusty creatures, showing themselves off in outfits which ought never to be allowed, not even for the purposes of entertainment. Anna hadn't heard much about God, but the one she knew of seemed a lot kinder than whoever Mrs Bunker beheld to. The mystery young man had followed God, and Anna had a hard time believing he would follow a Ruler who would be so cruel and vindictive.

Having no deformity and never having worn a performer's outfit herself, Anna wasn't quite sure where she fit in Mrs Bunker's description. However, as the months went by, it became clear that Mrs Bunker tarred all with the same brush. Anna had been part of the circus and was tainted by that same immorality, whatever part she had played in it.

"Yes, Mrs Bunker, right away," Anna said, lifting the heavy basketful of wet sheets, sheets she had herself washed before the sun had even come up. She hurried away into the fenced off yard where several lines were strung for the very purpose of drying the Leyland household laundry.

It was a nice and bright early spring day, a good drying day. It was breezy, even if there was a cool bite to the air. The sky was blue, with not a cloud anywhere, and as Anna hung the wet sheets, she felt a curious sense of contentment. She was sure it wouldn't last, for why would it? This was just a tiny moment in amongst so many other moments; other moments which did not lend themselves to contentment of any kind. She was, after all, a scullery maid; working her fingers to the bone from morning till night for the paltriest pay. The pay was so appalling that it was almost nothing, and certainly, she would have to save her money for a very long time to be able to buy anything of simple value such as stockings, or a new nightgown.

The truth was that her new life as a scullery maid served only one purpose, and that was to keep her alive. She had a roof over her head and food in her belly, the very same terms that she had worked for Mr Gerrity under. Still, at least she hadn't been out on the streets of London trying to stay warm over the winter. She had a bed, blankets, and even if she didn't seem to have prospects of any kind, she was safe and alive.

"You're a million miles away, lady! Penny for your thoughts?" The voice startled her, and she turned around sharply to see one of the young footmen, Jack Merritt.

"I'm busy, Jack," Anna said, wanting to put him off before he'd even begun.

Anna didn't like Jack Merritt very much. He was a little older than her, at nineteen, and at first glance, he was an extraordinarily handsome young man. He had bright blue eyes and pale blond hair, just as Lucy had. In fact, his colouring had reminded her so much of her dear departed friend that in her first few weeks working in the house on Cleaver Square, Anna had smiled at him more than once.

It had never been a smile of encouragement, nor of attraction. It was just a friendly smile, nothing more. However, as the months had passed, Anna had come to realise that Jack was of the breed of men who didn't need any encouragement. She might have smiled or scowled at him; it made no difference. Her own wants made no difference, just as her lack of attraction for him made no difference.

Of course, Anna had no real proof of this. It was entirely based upon her feelings for the man, her own instinct, and her already far too detailed experience of such things.

"You're always busy. I'm always busy," he said and gave her a broad and winning smile. "Doesn't mean we can't make time for a little fun, does it?"

"I don't think Mrs Bunker would be very pleased about the idea of the household servants having fun of any kind, Jack," Anna said a little sharply.

"Who cares what Mrs Bunker thinks, Anna? I'm not talking about Mrs Bunker, I'm talking about us," he said, and the bright and winning smile became something a little more lascivious.

"What do you mean *us?*" Anna said coldly; she'd had just about enough of men of his type. Her father had been one, as had Mr Gerrity; were they all the same?

"I think you know exactly what I mean. You're a circus girl, aren't you?" His eyes had a dangerous glint in them now.

"You don't know anything about the circus, just as you don't know anything about me. People are just people wherever you find them, whatever the setting. Yes, there are people of low morals in the circus, just as there are people of low morals right here in this very house!" She was scowling at him, wanting him to recognise the description of himself. "But there are good people too, clean and decent people, and I'm one of them. I have no interest in you, Jack, and I'm sorry that I ever smiled at you in friendship."

"That's just it, Anna, you *did* smile at me. You can't take it back now," he said and took a step towards her.

"What do you mean?" Anna asked, thinking that there was more to that sinister little sentence than met the eye. She had just one more sheet to hang, but her hands had begun to tremble, and she simply held onto it, as if it was some kind of fabric shield.

"You gave me the come on, you know you did," he said, still advancing upon her.

"Does nobody else ever smile at you, Jack? Or do you assume that everybody who smiles at you is inviting you to use them? You're a fool if that's what you think. And yes, I can take my smile back if I want; it's my smile!" She was furious and terrified at once. If she had to scream, she would, even if it was sure to draw Mrs Bunker's attention.

Of course, if she had to scream for help and Mrs Bunker got to hear of it, that dreadful old housekeeper would blame her.

"Come here, girl," Jack said, a horribly confident smile on his face, a swagger in his every footstep.

"Oi, you get away from her!" Little Billy Smith let himself in through the high gate in the fencing which enclosed the little yard. "Didn't you hear what she said? She doesn't want to talk to you, Merritt!"

"You little pipsqueak!" Jack said and started to laugh at the little boy.

"Leave him alone," Anna said, as keen to defend Billy as he had been keen to defend her; he was only just nine years old now and still so small, so brave.

"She's a bit old for you, son," Jack said and laughed.

"It ain't decent, Jack, the way you talk to girls." Billy squeaked.

"Well, aren't you the brave little gentleman?" Jack said, sneering.

He turned away from little Billy, as if the boy wasn't there at all, and continued to make his way towards Anna. Anna backed away until she collided with the high wooden fencing and had nowhere else to go. She felt nauseated, just as she had done that night when she was certain she wouldn't be able to escape Mr Gerrity. She seethed, but she was terrified, still clutching the wet sheet, holding it out in front of her.

"A little bit of linen won't save you, lady."

"Mrs Bunker will come out to look for me in a minute," Anna said, trying to talk her way out of it.

"Well, she ain't here now, is she?" Jack said and started to lean in towards her, trying to kiss her. "Ouch!" Suddenly, he cried out in pain and spun around. "You little gutter rat! You'll regret kicking me, child, I can promise you that!"

It was clear that Billy had kicked Jack to get him away from Anna, but now Jack was advancing upon the little boy, his face full of fury. Anna was certain that he would do the child harm. She wanted to run for help, but she knew that Mrs Bunker would find some way to blame the whole thing on her; the circus girl with low morals.

Just as Jack reached for Billy, the boy looking frightened but defiant, Anna had a flash of inspiration and threw the wet sheet over Jack's head. With him suitably blinded and fighting for escape from what must have seemed like acres of wet linen, Anna caught Billy's eye, and the two of them took the opportunity to each kick a shin at the same time, leaving Jack howling furiously as they ran away back into the servants' area and the safety of Mrs Bunker's scowling face.

"You took your time, Anna!" Mrs Bunker said waspishly.

"I'm sorry, Mrs Bunker," Anna said, trying to forget everything that had almost happened.

However, Anna had the greatest sense that she was on borrowed time. She knew men like Jack Merritt, she knew their pride, ego, and determination to have their needs met. Sooner or later, Jack Merritt would make her pay, nothing was surer.

CHAPTER 7

Some weeks later, Anna was sent out to the market at the Elephant and Castle to collect one or two items for Mrs Bunker. Even though Mrs Bunker had decided not to like Anna, and had already decided what she thought her standards to be... still, she seemed to trust her more than the rest of the scullery maids.

Perhaps it helped that Anna could read and write, perhaps it helped that she was a little older, taller, and much more capable looking than the other girls. Anna felt sorry for them all; they had clearly been born into and raised in poverty, everything about them proclaimed it. The dry hair and dull skin, their rotten teeth, their short stature. These were not girls who had been looked after, that was certain.

Anna realised that she'd been kept quite healthy in the circus. Perhaps it was because Mr Gerrity wanted to look after his assets, so to speak. Whilst the provisions had never been fancy, they had certainly been nutritious, and they had never been too scarce. Still, even with that much to recommend it, Anna knew that she would never, ever go back to the circus, *any circus*, ever again. She despised it, almost as much as she despised those who pulled their coins from their pockets so that they might enjoy the sight of every humiliation on offer.

It was a little warmer, and London seemed like a much more pleasant place in the sunshine. It was just a twenty-minute walk from Kennington to the market at the Elephant and Castle, and Anna enjoyed every moment of it.

When she walked past the big music hall, a fine building constructed in the Georgian style, her eye was drawn to one of the billboards. It was huge, almost half her height, and the letters proclaimed in bold black type that Miss Nellie March would be singing that night.

Anna had heard the name of Nellie March before; she'd heard one of the housemaids, the privileged breed of servant who worked upstairs rather than below stairs, talking about how her brother had taken her to the music hall. They'd even sat in the good seats, in amongst the smattering of fine ladies and gentlemen who enjoyed such entertainments. The housemaid had heard Nellie March sing and declared that she'd never heard anything more beautiful.

Anna stared up at the billboard, taking in every inch of Nellie March's appearance. It was a standard sort of poster, a woman in a fine dress holding up a parasol as if the sun itself might shine within the walls of that very music hall. Her hair must've been golden, or at least light, for it didn't look at all dark in the black and white print. Her dress looked pale too, and she stood against a dark background, a little table to one side of her, a beautiful vase of flowers expertly arranged.

"Don't miss Miss Nellie March, the sweetest singer in town," the billboard urged. In smaller print, it went on to state, "Also starring Miss Millie Chapel and her brother Archie, the most famous, breath-taking knife-throwing act in London!"

Anna read the rest of the huge billboard, boasting a female acrobat called Maisie Freeport, a vaudeville comedy duo, a strongman, a ventriloquist, musicians and dancers galore, and male and female impersonators. There was something so fresh about the line-up of performers that Anna couldn't take her eyes off the billboard.

The thing which struck her most was a seeming lack of cruelty. There were no caged animals, bearded women, or others struck with the cruellest of deformities. Of course, there were other music halls in London who boasted such acts, but Anna knew that they catered to the very most basic people in London. Why was it that those of her own class were often the cruellest? Perhaps they needed to kick downward; perhaps they needed to assure themselves that there were people in the world worse off than them, lower than them. Whatever it was, it sickened Anna.

Still, this particular establishment, somewhere between Kennington and the Elephant and Castle, seemed like the sort of place that little Billy Smith would have described as *upmarket*. So, Anna stared at Nellie March and wondered what it would feel like to be so admired, to be such a wonderful singer. For a start, she doubted Nellie March was sent on errands to the market at the Elephant and Castle, nor, did Anna imagine, that Nellie March had a great pile of carrots and potatoes waiting for her when she returned, each and every one of them needing peeling.

In this moment, Anna was struck by the poignant memory of Lucy talking about her dream. It felt like twenty-years ago, but was it really only two? As Anna looked up at the billboard, she could feel the rumblings of a dream rising in her own chest. To sing and perform on that stage, a crowd of adoring fans, no threat of harm during or after the show. That would be the life. She breathed in the dream.

"Good luck to you, Nellie March," Anna said under her breath, smiling at the unmoving, sightless woman who peered out from the billboard.

∽

When Anna returned from her errands at the Elephant and Castle market, she did indeed have a huge basket of vegetables waiting for her, all of which needed preparing for the family's dinner that evening.

There was no sign of Mrs Bunker anywhere, so she made her way to the scullery with the basket which she took from the kitchen table. Knowing there was no time like the present, she might just as well get started.

With her thick cotton apron tied around her, Anna began to peel carrots. After a minute or two, she realised she was humming, something that she hadn't done for a very long time. She didn't feel any happier than she had the day before or even the day before that, and she realised that there was no particular reason for the humming beyond the fact that she had become so mesmerised by the billboard poster of Nellie March.

When she'd peeled the first load of carrots, Anna dumped them into the bowl of salted water, moving them about, cleaning off any little bits of peel that still clung. The salt made her hands sting dreadfully, and she quickly withdrew them from the water and dried them on the front of the apron. She studied them, seeing how red and irritated they were.

Perhaps it was because her hands seemed to be plunged into water all day long. If she wasn't washing vegetables, washing plates and cups and pans, then she was washing sheets and shirts and everything else that the Leyland family seemed to use in great measure.

There was only Mr and Mrs Leyland and one grown-up son, people she hardly ever set eyes on. Confined always to the world below stairs, Anna had never served the family tea, nor had she done a little dusting or set fires in the grates in the drawing room. She had only seen the family twice, and on each occasion, she had been making her way to the Elephant and Castle running errands for Mrs Bunker.

They looked pleasant enough, although they did, of course, ignore her entirely. She still wondered how it was that just three people could require so many others to look after them. When she'd been with Mr Garrity's circus, Anna had had to attend to the needs of so many, all on her own. There had been so many performers she couldn't count them, not to mention the animals which needed feeding. Yet, here was the Leyland family, just three of them and a small stable to house their carriage and a few horses. They were greatly outnumbered by the servants who worked from dawn until dusk to see to their every need. What a strange country this was. What a peculiar place where people existed who did not know instinctively how to look after themselves.

"Staring at your hands won't get the carrots peeled, will it?" Jack Merritt walked into the room, a victorious smile on his face.

"Neither will talking, if you'll excuse me," she said, and picked up a potato and the small knife she used for peeling.

Anna strained to listen, hoping to hear the cook in the kitchen, or Mrs Bunker, or anybody at all, but she heard nothing. She had managed to avoid Jack for weeks and weeks now, enjoying a sort of temporary safety, but Anna realised that safety had come to an end. Jack was going to make her pay for his small humiliation out in the yard. She gripped the little peeling knife tighter.

"Funny really, you thinking you're so much better than everybody else. Your prim little ways, your neat brown hair," he said, mocking her. "That apron tied tight, your back straight, your head held high," he went on.

"Is there any reason why my back shouldn't be straight, Jack?" she said, knowing that to react to his insults wouldn't help her, but unable to stop herself. What an ugly young man he was! How had he once looked so pleasing, so handsome to her? There was something in his face which made a mockery of those beautiful bright blue eyes and that impossibly light blonde hair. It was as if, without even trying, he was taunting her for the loss of her old friend, the loss of Lucy Lawrence, the Flying Fairy.

"You think you're better than us!" Jack went on, taunting her.

"I don't think I'm better than anybody, but I don't think I'm lower than anybody either."

"I don't think I've ever met a girl who needs teaching a lesson more than you do, Anna Bailey! A jumped-up little circus girl!" This time, he didn't creep up on her, he darted across the room enclosing her into the corner. "And don't lie. We all get lonely sometimes. Maybe that's why you're so stuck-up, ever thought of that?"

Anna was still clutching the potato and the knife, both down by her sides. When she realised that her first instinct had been to drive the little peeling knife into Jack's chest, her breathing became ragged, and she felt hot and sick. If it came to it, would she really do it? If Jack was going to get away with anything he wanted, would she really stop him in so deadly a way?

Anna's heart was pounding, and her anger boiling horribly within her. She turned her face away from him as he took another step closer to her. She could feel his hot breathe on her face now, see his hands twitching. She adjusted her grip on the little knife and knew that if she didn't cry out soon, if somebody didn't come, then she would surely kill him. Well, she wouldn't go to the gallows for a worthless lowdown little monster like Jack Merritt, that was for sure.

For the second time in her life, Anna used her own voice as a weapon in the worst of situations. As calmly as she could, she slowed her breathing and then carefully drew in so much air that her lungs were full to bursting before she let out the most bloodcurdling scream for help.

Footsteps came much faster than she had expected, and the door to the scullery was flung open.

Anna's head was still turned to the side, and she looked beseechingly at Mrs Bunker as she strode into the room.

"Please help me, Mrs Bunker," Anna said, tears streaming down her face. However, Mrs Bunker simply glared at her.

"Jack, don't you have work to be doing somewhere else?" Mrs Bunker said, her voice annoyed, but her glare lavished only on Anna.

"Yes, Mrs Bunker," Jack said and hurried away.

"Thank you, it's the second time he's tried to do this, Mrs Bunker, and I can't bear him. I'm so afraid of him."

"So you say," Mrs Bunker said, standing there with her arms folded across her chest and a gleefully disapproving look on her face. This was just the very moment that Mrs Bunker had been waiting for, the moment which would make all her assertions that all circus folk had low morals absolutely correct. It didn't matter that she knew, and it was *clear* that she did, that Anna was not to blame. This was an opportunity to be right that Mrs Bunker wasn't going to let go of.

"So I say, and it is the truth, Mrs Bunker!" Anna set down the potato and the knife with shaking hands. "You may ask Billy Smith if you need a witness, Mrs Bunker. He had to rescue me one day in the yard when Jack was pestering me in just the same way. It isn't right that he gets away with it."

"And it isn't for you, a simple scullery maid, to tell the housekeeper how to go about her business. Jack Merritt is a fine young man with a good future ahead of him. He is already a footman at his tender age, and I have no doubt that he will make it all the way to butler one day. But what about you, Anna Bailey? What about you, a good-for-nothing circus girl with no morals? Just how far do you expect to make it in this world without resorting to what I've seen with my own eyes today?"

"You know what you saw with your own eyes, Mrs Bunker!" Anna said, holding back the sob that was caught in her throat. "You know what you've seen, but you will always side with the men. I would never do that to another woman, so which of us really is the one with low morals?" She was furious, so furious that she wanted to slap the ageing housekeeper.

"Well, we'll just see what Mrs Leyland has to say about it all!" Mrs Bunker said, clearly insulted, before turning on her heel and marching out of the scullery.

CHAPTER 8

Mrs Bunker, as housekeeper, could have dismissed Anna without any consultation with her mistress. It was for her to hire and fire simple scullery maids, but she had chosen not to do that, and Anna knew why; the woman wanted the whole song and dance. She wanted to be raised up in the estimations of her mistress; to be thought of as a fine woman of high morals and standards. How would her mistress see her in such a light if she did not first bring to her attention the dreadful behaviour of Anna Bailey? Once again, Anna was to be the sideshow, mocked and humiliated.

The whole business was dragged on far longer than it ought to have been, for Mr and Mrs Leyland were entertaining a guest out in their beautiful terraced garden at the back of the house. It was mid-afternoon, and they were taking tea. Anna could hear them talking in the distance, a low rumble of conversation with no discernible words, as she pegged out yet more freshly washed sheets. It seemed that Mrs Bunker was to get every ounce of work from the girl before taking great delight in dismissing her. Anna had to fight the urge to raise her voice and attempt to defend herself and her dignity. She was smart enough to know that any resistance she would make, could be twisted and thrown right back into her face by Mrs Bunker.

The afternoon was warm, and the sky still a wonderfully clear blue. It had seemed an age since she'd gazed upon the picture of Nelly March on the billboard outside the music hall, almost a lifetime ago. But wasn't it always the way? A day could start off one way and end as something entirely different. One minute she was content doing errands, the next she was facing destitution once again. It was so tiring, life, and she closed her eyes, remembering that awful moment when Lucy simply let go of the trapeze bar. Let go of her dream.

As she continued to peg out the washing, Anna began to sing. She felt desperate and hopeless, realising that she had nowhere to turn, no one to turn to, and she never would. She closed her eyes for a moment, the sun on her face, and began to sing.

"Tears, idle tears, I know not what they mean,

Tears from the depth of some divine despair

Rise in the heart, and gather to the eyes,

In looking on the happy Autumn fields,

And thinking of the days that are no more."

Tears rolled down her face, and she didn't bother to wipe them away; she simply stood there, waiting for life to swallow her whole once again. She was so lost in her own thoughts that she didn't hear the gate in the fence opening, nor did she hear the soft footsteps of the man who had let himself into the little yard.

"I knew it! I knew it was you!" The man's voice suddenly brought her world back into sharp focus, and she opened her eyes to find herself staring at a face she recognised. Where did she know him from? What was he doing here?

"As soon as I heard that song, that wonderful voice, I knew it was the little Nightingale." He smiled at her, and suddenly she knew him; it was the man who had spoken to her in the animal enclosure, the man who had been the catalyst for everything which had followed.

However, she didn't blame the man for any of it; he couldn't have known, and it certainly wasn't his fault. All he had done on that day was compliment her singing, Mr Gerrity had done the rest.

"I remember you from the circus, sir," she said, realising that she didn't know his name.

"And I remember you, Nightingale." He laughed. "I suppose that is a little rude to call you that, although please know that I mean it most genuinely and kindly. Tell me, what is your name?"

"I am Anna, sir. Anna Bailey."

"And how is it you find yourself here, working for Mr and Mrs Leyland?" He seemed genuinely interested and, despite the question she had about what he was doing there, she could do no other than answer him.

"I was cast out of the circus, sir, by Mr Gerrity and his wife. Though in many ways, it was the day I gained my freedom too." She wistfully hung up another shirt.

"That ringmaster had a dreadful temper, I think," he said, looking truly disquieted for a moment. "I hope it was not my sudden appearance in the animal enclosure which saw you cast out, Miss Bailey?" She could see in his eyes that he wanted to be assured that she had come to no harm on account of his actions.

"Mr Gerrity has a temper as you say, sir, but it could be excited by anything. It was just a matter of time, I suppose, until something happened…"

"He didn't hurt you, did he?"

"He tried, but he didn't succeed," Anna said and stared into his pale blue eyes.

"And you came directly here?"

"Yes, I was very fortunate to meet a child who told me that the housekeeper was in want of a new scullery maid. I daresay it is a position the housekeeper finds herself in regularly," she said, determined not to hold back her bile where Mrs Bunker was concerned; what did she have to lose now?

"And how do you like working here?"

"It's not so very different from the circus. I work from sun-up till sundown, breaking my back for people who either don't realise I exist and wouldn't care if they did. Forgive me, but that is the truth of it. That is how I feel, Mr…?"

"Warner, Jonathan Warner," he said and inclined his head a little, a curiously respectful gesture.

"Well, Mr Warner, I suppose you're a friend of Mr and Mrs Leyland?"

"Not exactly," he said in a whisper and looked over his shoulder before turning back to her. "The truth is, I'm trying to convince them to spend an evening or two in my music hall. Free of charge, of course, but it would help me out greatly."

"Why?"

"I run a very decent sort of music hall, Miss Bailey, and I would like all of London to know it. I get one or two patrons of a higher class, but not as many as I'd like. I want my music hall to appeal to everybody, to be open to everybody. However, Mr and Mrs Leyland think the whole thing beneath them," he said and shrugged.

"Beneath them?"

"Yes, Mrs Leyland made no secret of the fact that she thinks the music hall is like the circus. Meant for people of a lower class and a lower intellect, apparently," he shook his head and narrowed his eyes a little bitterly.

"Until she is confronted with a man whose head is too small for his body or a woman with too much hair on her face. Mark my words, she'll stop and stare like all the rest, no doubt about it," she said, a look of disgust on her face. "There's *thinking* you're better and there's *being* better."

"I agree, Miss Bailey, although I am bound to point out that I have no sideshows at my music hall. God teaches kindness, not cruelty. It is proper entertainment, decent entertainment."

"Yes, I know. I've seen the billboard. You have a singer, Nellie March, she looks very pretty."

"She's a very good singer, my patrons seem to adore her. However, she is no longer Nellie March, but Mrs Nellie Wainwright. Her husband doesn't want her singing anymore, not in public," he said and shook his head. "Hypocritical really, since the music hall is where he met her."

"I often find men can be a little hypocritical. But in truth, I find women can be a little hypocritical also," she shrugged, and he laughed.

"Tell me, do you often sing?" He changed the subject.

"I rarely sing, Mr Warner. The only time I have sung this way in the last years seems to be when you were within earshot."

"Your voice is so wonderfully emotional, I can feel it in my heart," he said, surprising her with his words and the fact that he didn't seem at all embarrassed by them. "You are an artist, no doubt about it, but I think an unintentional one. What made you so sad today that you sang so beautifully?"

"It's a tale that doesn't really bear repeating, sir," Anna said and shook her head.

"Did something happen?"

"Ever since I have worked here, one of the footmen has been pestering me." She paused for long enough that she was certain he understood her meaning without her having to spell it out. "I've managed to stay out of his way as best I can, but today he had me cornered, and I was so afraid that I cried out for help. Mrs Bunker, the housekeeper, blames me for it, of course. She's going to speak to Mrs Leyland this afternoon and see about having me dismissed."

"But surely, she could see it wasn't your fault? You were the one who cried out after all, weren't you?"

"Of course, she could see it wasn't my fault," Anna said, surprising herself with a cynical laugh. "But that doesn't matter to Mrs Bunker. All that matters is that she thinks she's been proved right; the circus girl is of low morals, just as she always thought, and now she has her proof for all to see."

"But that's appalling," Mr Warner said and shook his head.

"It is, but I'm sure you know, Mr Warner, that people seem to find it easier to blame women than to blame men for such things, don't they?" She was holding his gaze now, almost challenging him to disagree with her.

"You're right, but it's still appalling." He looked down at his feet for a moment before raising his head and smiling brightly. "I say, do you believe that prayers can be answered?"

"Can't say I've ever even prayed, sir, let alone had one answered," she said, and he laughed.

"Well, you see, imagine us meeting today of all days. I am about to lose my best singer, and you are potentially about to lose your position here. I've been praying for some sort of answer, a way to get Nellie back, or someone to take her place and… I know you to be so fine a singer that you will surely touch everybody's hearts. What do you say, Miss Anna Bailey? Will you come and work for me in the music hall? An answer to my prayers?"

"Yes," Anna said before she knew it. For a moment, she wondered about taking it back, knowing that it was a risky move. She didn't know this man; she didn't know what it was he wanted of her.

However, certain that she was about to find herself cast out onto the streets of London once more, what choice did she have? Anyway, being the answer to Mr Warner's prayers didn't sound so bad.

CHAPTER 9

"So, you walked out before she could give you your marching orders?!" Maisy Freeport, an acrobat and burgeoning juggler, looked at Anna with wide-eyed admiration.

"I suppose you could say that," Anna said, feeling a little overwhelmed by the young woman's undivided attention.

Anna had only moved into her room upstairs in the music hall the evening before, and already Maisy had extracted a great deal of her life's story from her. Still, Maisy was pleasant and friendly, something which Anna hadn't experienced for a good long while.

She thought of little Billy Smith; he'd been pleasant and friendly, hadn't he? It hurt her heart to think of how she'd had to say goodbye to him. He was a brave and self-assured little boy, but she could tell from the look in his eyes that he was sad to see her go.

Mrs Bunker's face, on the other hand, had been a real sight for sore eyes. Robbed of her chance to shine as an example of morals for the entire household, Mrs Bunker was furious to be told that she was not only being given notice of Anna's intention to depart but that she would be leaving that very day. There would be no time for Mrs Bunker to run to the mistress of the house with her made up tales of the wicked servant girl after all. When she'd declared that Anna would get no reference from the mistress and had received nothing more than a nonchalant shrug in return, Mrs Bunker had turned bright red and looked most unsteady; pure anger really didn't suit the woman.

Neither did cockiness suit Anna and she made a mental note not to make a habit of indulging herself in that way. She would make Mrs Bunker the exception. She'd had her moment of satisfaction but now had come the time to fulfil *her* part of the bargain. But how on earth was she to sing before such a large audience? She'd never sung before anybody in her life. Apart from Mr Warner, of course, and *that* had been unintentional.

"I'll bet the old bat didn't like that much!" Maisie said and laughed. "I bet you took the wind right out of her sails."

"I suppose I did," Anna said, but her voice was vague and her mind already wandering along the uncertain path of what lay ahead.

"What's the matter?" Maisie asked, making herself entirely at home in the room Jonathan Warner had given Anna to live in.

Maisie was in the room next door, and the two rooms seemed to be of a similar size and decorated to a similar standard. Anna had never stayed anywhere so nice before, and certainly, she had never had so much space. The room was a big square and had a bed, a wardrobe, a dressing table with a mirror on it and a little stool tucked beneath a washstand, and a rail which Maisie had already told her would be where she hung her outfits for the show.

Inside the dresser was a small book too, and under closer inspection Anna had found it to be a Bible. She had leafed through it the first night she had come, not entirely sure what she was looking for. She had found a line that really stood out to her: 'Peace I leave with you, my peace I give unto you: not as the world giveth, give I unto you. Let not your heart be troubled, neither let it be afraid.' Right now though, all she felt was panic.

"I don't know if I can do it, Maisie. I'm not a singer, not really. I mean, Mr Warner thinks I can sing, but I'm not a professional singer. I don't know how I'm going to stand there in front of an audience and sing, I'd just be too nervous."

"You'll be nervous at first, but you'll get over it. I know I did. The first night I performed on stage, I was so nervous that I came out of a somersault and landed flat on my backside. The audience didn't seem to mind," she said, making Anna laugh. "In fact, I think it's the closest to a standing ovation I ever got!"

"You are funny, Maisie," Anna said, feeling a little better but having that gnawing sensation in her stomach; a sensation which told her that she still had a mountain to climb. "Mr Warner has been so kind; I don't want to let him down."

"He's been kind, and he'll stay kind, Anna. He's a decent man, believe it or not. I know, a rarity in our business."

"Yes, he's not at all what I expected of somebody running a music hall."

"He's an educated man, right enough. He's a gentleman, brought up as one and everything. And his father was a gentleman before him, so I suppose you could say Mr Warner has a good pedigree. Anyway, it was the old man who owned the place, a real lover of the old vaudeville acts, he was. Anyway, Mr Warner has a good eye for the arts, and he likes the show to be something a little bit more decent, a bit more upmarket than some of the others."

"That makes a nice change. I must admit, it was a relief not to see any sideshow acts on the billboard."

"Don't you like the sideshows?"

"I was raised in the circus, and I've seen enough heartbreaking sideshows to last me a lifetime."

"Yes, I think it's a little bit cruel, isn't it? Laughing and pointing at people who've already got their cross to bear." Maisie was so genuine that Anna knew she was going to like her very much indeed.

"It is, I hate it."

"But it must have been wonderful being in the circus, wasn't it? I'd give anything to be an Acrobat in the circus. And I'm learning to juggle too! As soon as I get the hang of it, Mr Warner says I can add a little juggling to my act."

"That's wonderful!" Anna smiled at her. "But please, don't ever think of leaving the music hall for the circus. It's not an easy way of life. You don't have any roots or home, no friends you can turn to, nobody to rely on. That travelling lifestyle makes you more vulnerable to some very unpleasant people. Well, men, mostly."

"Maybe the grass is greener right here then?"

"Oh, yes, without a doubt."

"Come on, let's go and have a look at the hall. It's still early, and nobody will be rehearsing yet, so we'll have the place to ourselves for a little while. It might help to get rid of your nerves," Maisie said and reached out for her hand. Anna took it and allowed the pretty young Acrobat to lead her through a maze of corridors to the stairs and down into the main part of the music hall.

However, when they arrived on the stage, Anna felt worse, not better. It was huge; the great wide stage with beautiful velvet curtains, the orchestra pit on one side, and seating everywhere.

"There's no standing area," Anna said, finding something to say as a way of making her feel normal, of planting her nervous feet firmly on the ground.

"No, Mr Warner doesn't like that. He lets everybody in, of course, and there are cheaper seats, but there's no standing. He said it's like a bear pit otherwise. But the cheaper seats are very reasonable, not very much more than somebody might pay to stand in one of the other, not so nice, music halls."

"It's just so big," Anna said and wondered how her tiny voice was to make its way across such a large space, all the way to the back and up into the gilt-painted balconies. She felt tearful and panic-stricken; she couldn't do this.

"Are you all right?"

"No, I'm not all right, Maisie. I've made a terrible, terrible mistake. When Mr Warner finds out that I can't sing, that I can't manage this in front of so many people, he's going to be furious. He's going to throw me out, and I'll be right back where I started. Oh, what have I done?" She spoke the last more to herself than anybody else, and finally, her tears began to fall.

"Well, you most certainly can sing, Anna." Mr Warner walked onto the stage from the wings, smiling warmly at her. "And everybody gets nervous, this is a big hall. I'm not expecting you to go out there tonight, and sing your heart out. It's going to take time and practice, but there's no rush."

"Oh, Mr Warner," Anna said, pulling a handkerchief from her sleeve and quickly drying her face. "I'm sorry, you must think me so ungrateful."

"I don't think you ungrateful at all. And anyway, it was I who approached you, wasn't it? You haven't asked me for a single thing. If it makes you feel any better, I know already that you have the sort of voice which will draw crowds from all over London once you get going. So, it's probably for me to be grateful to you and not the other way around." He smiled at her again, and it brought tears to her eyes once more.

Nobody had ever been that kind to her, not since Lucy Lawrence had died. Even though she wasn't entirely sure she believed him about the power of her voice, still, his words had somehow given her confidence, made her stand straighter and taller.

"I'll practice with you," he went on when it was clear she couldn't speak. "We'll start small and work our way up, all right? We'll practice early in the morning before the other performers begin to practice and then, as your confidence grows, you can do a little singing in front of them, can't she, Maisie?" He turned to Maisie and smiled, drawing her into the conversation.

"Of course! You just need to find your feet, that's all. It's the same for everybody who performs, there's always that first time to get through, isn't there?" Maisie said helpfully.

"That really is so kind of you. Both of you," she said, sniffing as she looked from one to the other. "I just hope I don't let you down."

"You won't, don't worry," Mr Warner said, his pale blue eyes kind, his face young and handsome. "So, what do you say? Shall we start tomorrow morning after breakfast?"

CHAPTER 10

All in all, Anna could hardly believe her luck. She'd been living at the music hall for three weeks, and she had enjoyed every bit of it. She still couldn't get used to the fact that, for the few performers who lived in rooms above the hall, there was a kindly housekeeper who provided their meals. They had to keep their own rooms clean and do their own laundry, but that was far from a hardship to a girl who'd done that all her life.

True to his word, Jonathan Warner had practised with her every morning right after breakfast. He played the piano whilst she sang, so many of the songs she already knew by heart. She'd been shy and embarrassed at first. Jonathan had simply told her to stand with her back to him, or even to close her eyes, whatever it took to make her feel as if she was singing by herself, pegging out washing with her heart broken and every emotion infusing the melody. And it worked too; even Anna was starting to believe that she could not only sing but sing extraordinarily well.

"So, how do you feel?" he said on her last practice before her debut in the show. "Nervous?"

"Terrified," Anna said and gave a self-deprecating laugh. "But I can do it, I promise."

"You've already become accustomed to singing in front of the rest of the performers, and they most certainly are a picky bunch, much pickier than any of the audience will be. So, if they love you, then the audience will. There, that should give you a little more confidence, shouldn't it?" He was sitting at the piano, his shirt sleeves rolled up and his necktie in his pocket. He still looked smart with his waistcoat and fine trousers and shoes, but the lack of formality made him look young, boyish and approachable. Anna liked him more and more.

"They've all been so kind," Anna said, knowing there was a stark difference between the people she worked with now and the people at the circus; they were less hard somehow, more encouraging.

The circus performers were extraordinary in their abilities, there was no doubt about it. The Acrobats seemed to know no fear, their performances so much more death-defying than anything Maisie Freeport displayed. Maisie was a good Acrobat, making great use of the space on the stage and wowing the audience night after night with her elegance and strength. However, there was nothing about her performance that might lead to her death; that wasn't the sort of show that Mr Jonathan Warner put on.

Perhaps that was why circus performers were hard and harsh in their attitude to everything in life, even each other. They were jaded, cynical, and very rarely supportive of one another. The only truly kind soul Anna had ever known in a lifetime of travelling with *Gerrity's Unbelievable Show* had been Lucy Lawrence. Without a doubt, that was why she had loved her like a big sister.

"They are kind, Anna, but they are also honest. If they didn't think you were ready, they would tell it to you for your own good. And if I didn't think you were ready, I wouldn't let you go out there. I wouldn't do that to you," he said, his voice suddenly low and intent. It did something to her; it created an unfamiliar sensation in her chest.

"Thank you," she said, feeling her cheeks warm a little, though whether from the praise or that sudden strange feeling of closeness, she couldn't have said.

"So, spend the rest of the day relaxing. Take naps, read, anything that will keep you nice and calm and rested." He got up from behind the piano and pulled his necktie out of his pocket, straightening his collars and tying it on expertly. He unrolled his sleeves and picked up his smart coat, putting it on and looking every inch the fine gentleman.

"I will, Mr Warner, thank you." Anna turned to leave, but hesitated. "Mr Warner?"

He looked up from the piano. "Yes?"

"Are you…" Anna felt her cheeks flush red again. "Are you still praying for me?"

Johnathan's face broke out in a warm smile. "Of course I am, Anna. I never stopped, ever since I met you."

Anna felt her heart skip a beat. "Thank you, truly."

∼

Standing in the wings that evening, Anna looked down at her dress. It was a beautiful dress made from ivory cotton and silk, the trim at the neckline was lace, and there were great cuffs of lace which hung loose and elegant around her wrists. She'd never worn such a gown in her life, nor had she had her hair curled and piled up in such a sophisticated way.

When she first tried on the dress, Anna had been so excited she could barely speak. Now, looking down at herself, it was the *reason* for the dress which was turning her inside out. Mr Warner had bought her a fine dress so that she would be ready to put on a fine performance. But her hands were shaking, her heart was pounding, and she felt sick. She had peeked out from behind the curtain at the wing of the stage and seen that so many of the seats were occupied. It wasn't a full house, apparently, that was something that Mr Warner was still striving for, but there were so, so many people.

"Are you ready?" From nowhere, Jonathan Warner was suddenly at her side. He looked wonderful in a fine dress suit with top hat and tails, ready to go out and announce the brand-new singer, Miss Anna Bailey.

"Yes," Anna said, but she knew she wasn't. Her mouth was dry, and her throat ached; she knew she would barely be able to croak the first line of the song she knew so well.

"Just remember, if it gets too much, just close your eyes. Close your eyes and see yourself hanging out the washing, feel yourself there with the sun on your face and a nice little breeze on your skin. Imagine you're all alone, nobody else to listen, and sing from the heart. The Lord is there to give you peace. Lean on him." He took her hand and squeezed it, smiling at her warmly. He was so kind; how could she do this to him? How could she let him down so badly?

As the last act finished, and Mr Warner took his first step towards the curtain, Anna reached out and seized his wrist. He turned to look at her, seeing the tears rolling down her face.

"I'm sorry, I can't. I just can't," she said, feeling devastated and ashamed as she turned to run from him.

Anna had charged up the stairs, running through the corridors until she was breathless with exertion and tears. She ran into her room and slammed the door behind her, throwing herself down on her little bed and wishing that the floor would open and swallow her whole. She'd let him down, and she couldn't begin to imagine how he was going to manage the audience now.

She had been lying face down some ten minutes before the door to her room finally opened.

"Anna? May I come in?" It was Mr Warner, and Anna knew what was coming. She sat up straight, perched on the edge of the bed, her hands in her lap, her head bowed. He was going to cast her out, and she didn't blame him for a minute.

"Are you all right?" he asked when she didn't speak. He came further into the room, leaving the door wide open behind him.

"I'm so sorry, Mr Warner. I should have been more honest; I should have told you from the very first that I have no talent, that I can't do this."

"Anna, please," he said and sat down on the bed beside her.

"I know I don't deserve it, sir, but could I stay here just one more night? I'll get my things together and leave in the morning."

"Leave?" he said, sounding utterly amazed. "Did you think that's what I'd come here to do? To throw you out?"

"I didn't do my job, sir, of course, you must throw me out. I don't blame you; I blame myself. This is my doing, my fault. This is why my father never trained me for anything in the circus; he said he knew by looking at me that I didn't have any talent, and he was right. I should have told you that in the beginning, Mr Warner. I should have..." she said and paused, dabbing her eyes with her handkerchief.

"Anna, I asked you to come here, and I would never dream of treating you that way. I don't know Kelvin Gerrity, but I know of his reputation. I know he is a harsh and unfair man like so many ringmasters in the circus business, but you're not in the circus now. You're here in my music hall, Anna, and I don't abandon people so easily."

"I don't understand, sir. How can there be a place for me here if I can't sing?" she asked, her mind working ten to the dozen and finally falling upon a solution. "But I can clean! I can clean and I can wash everybody's costumes. I can cook, I could even help the housekeeper with breakfast and dinner and anything you like. I'll even clean the windows, anything, any job at all." She was speaking hurriedly now, excitedly. Was this a way for her to stay alive, to keep a roof over her head and food in her belly?

"Thank you for the kind offer," Mr Warner said and started to laugh. "But I am afraid you are far too talented a young woman to be scrubbing windows and peeling potatoes.

"How can you say that now, sir? How can you say that when I just left you in the most awful predicament?"

"It really wasn't so awful, my dear, these things happen. And anyway, I let Maisie go out and have a go at her juggling act, so she's thrilled."

"She is?"

"She is! She didn't drop a single ball, and the crowd loved her. The ventriloquist is on now, and I told him to drag it out a little bit, so the audience will be getting their money's worth. You were only doing one song, Anna, it really isn't the end of the world. And you didn't let *me* down, I let *you* down. I pushed you and you weren't ready. But this is just one small stumble, Anna, not the end of the race. You just pick yourself up, dust yourself off, and start again."

Anna turned her head and looked at him, their eyes locked for some moments.

"But what if I can't ever do it? What then?"

"Don't look so far into the future. Don't dismiss yourself so easily. I don't care if your father told you that you didn't have any talent; I'm telling you that you have. I have never heard a voice as sweet and beautiful as yours, and I don't expect I'll ever hear anything like it again." He laughed gently for a moment, taking her hand between both of his and holding it. "And if, in the end, if you really can't manage going out onto the stage, then there are always the windows, aren't there?" He gave her a boyish grin, making her laugh.

They sat that way for some moments, her hand in his as they stared at one another intently. Finally, he leaned forward and kissed her. It wasn't a passionate kiss, but it was the first kiss she'd ever had in her life. He kissed on the lips, not the cheek, and Anna knew that *that* meant something. Her head was spinning, and when he drew away, Anna wanted nothing more than for him to lean forward and gently kiss her again.

"Anna, I really am so very sorry," he said and suddenly got to his feet, his face a picture of mortification. "I shouldn't have done that, I really shouldn't. Please, do forgive me for that. I would tell you I got caught up in the moment but that would be to excuse myself and I have no intentions of doing so. I promise you that I shall never do anything of that nature again, really. I hope you can find a way to forgive my appalling behaviour."

"Please don't worry about it, Mr Warner," Anna said, trying to get her bearings and feeling dreadfully confused; did he not like her? Or was he just such a gentleman? Choosing to see it as the latter, Anna realised she had never met such a fine man in all her life, nor had she ever expected to. In her mind, men were people like her father, or Mr Gerrity, or the dreadful little Jack Merritt. They were predators, horrible carnal creatures, determined to take what they wanted without asking. Now here he was, a fine and handsome young man whom any woman would surely be glad to be kissed by, and he was apologising for his behaviour.

"Mr Warner, I think I'd like to sing now if there's still time?" she said, that kiss filling her with both emotion and confidence. She didn't know how or why, but now was not the time to examine it. Now was the time to sing for Jonathan Warner.

∼

By default, Anna was the very final act of the evening. She waited in the wings and watched as Jonathan strode out to introduce her, looking so handsome it was enough to stop any young woman's heart. In that final moment, before she walked out onto the stage, he looked at her, his eyebrows slightly raised. She nodded at him, and he turned back to the audience.

"And now, ladies and gentlemen, Kennington's very own Nightingale, Miss Anna Bailey," he said and held out an arm in her direction. Anna walked out onto the stage, her face freshly washed, with no hint of the upset of the night.

She felt wonderful in her ivory gown, her chocolate brown hair soft and beautifully arranged, her breathing calm and steady. She nodded her thanks to Jonathan, who finally, somewhat reluctantly, vacated the stage. She looked down into the orchestra pit, smiling at the musicians, and took a deep breath. She nodded at the conductor and he raised his arms; the band began to play.

"Tears, idle tears, I know not what they mean,

Tears from the depth of some divine despair

Rise in the heart, and gather to the eyes,

In looking on the happy Autumn fields,

And thinking of the days that are no more..."

By the time she'd finished singing, Anna had realised that she had forgotten all about the audience. She had closed her eyes on occasion, almost seeing her own hands in front of her as they hung the washing on the line. Oh, and she had sung her little heart out, for the audience was suddenly on their feet and the applause and cheering was almost frightening in its volume and intensity.

Anna Bailey had brought the house down!

CHAPTER 11

In the months which followed, Anna had become something of a sensation in South London. Jonathan Warner finally achieved the thing he'd wanted; a full house. Not only was the house so often full, but it was a truly mixed crowd at last, with some very fine ladies and gentlemen gracing the lower circle with their presence.

It was a cold winter's morning when Anna wrapped herself up warmly in a fine wool cloak she'd bought with her earnings. She walked out of the hall, determined to have a walk down to the river. She paused by the front door, turning to look up at the billboard. There she was looking back at herself; a wonderful photograph of Anna wearing the fine ivory dress she'd worn that first night, carrying a parasol as she stood next to a beautiful vase of flowers on a little table.

Anna would never forget being in the photographer's studio; she'd never imagined ever having her photograph taken, much less ever seeing it up on a billboard in London.

Her voice really was wonderful, and now she had the confidence to gracefully accept the gift with which she had been so blessed. But it wasn't only her voice; her life felt blessed at last. She wasn't the girl who washed clothes and fed raw meat to the tigers anymore; she was fast becoming the Toast of London.

With a sense of all being right in her world, Anna set off for her walk with a smile on her face.

∽

"The boy I love is up in the gallery,

The boy I love is looking now at me,

There he is, can't you see, waving his handkerchief,

As merry as a robin that sings on a tree..."

As she sang that night, Anna could see she had the audience in the palm of her hand. She loved this song, it was so silly and so much fun, and she liked to see how the audience mouthed the words of that music-hall favourite, singing along with her.

It was so rare that she needed to close her eyes anymore to connect with the emotion within, or to block out the audience who had so kindly come to see her. Anna was at home now; she was comfortable with her talent. She understood it now.

She had a ritual she performed before each performance now. Alongside vocal exercises that would warm up her voice as well as calm her, she would read a passage or two from the Bible Mr Warner had given to her. She had summoned up the courage to ask him if there were any specific verses he particularly liked, and he was overjoyed to let her know some of his favourites. She made sure to write those down.

She looked around, scanning the faces for any sign of Jonathan. He so often wandered out into the crowd, taking a vacant seat somewhere to enjoy the performance from the audience's perspective. She noted that he mostly indulged himself in this little ritual when the performer on stage was Anna herself.

"The boy I love is up in the gallery,

The boy I love is looking now at me..." she continued, adoring this part of the song, always hoping to see Jonathan looking at her at that very moment. What would life be like if he really did love her?

As the months had gone by, Anna had found herself more and more drawn to him. She'd never been able to forget that brief, chaste little kiss that night when he had apologised so profusely. Of course, it never happened again, just as he'd promised, but Anna couldn't help but wish that it might, one day in the future. She got along very nicely with Jonathan Warner, and the two of them still practised after breakfast most mornings, even though there wasn't a need for it anymore. With her fear all gone, Anna could just as easily have practised with the rest of the performers later on in the day, and yet it seemed that this was just another little ritual, a ritual that they both indulged in. She hoped it wasn't simply a habit; she hoped it meant something more.

As the song drew to a close, Anna was disappointed not to have found Jonathan out in the crowd. However, as she took a bow, her eyes fell upon a face she recognised.

Of all the people in the world, she might have expected to see in the audience, her father, Bernard Bailey, was not chief among them. She drew her breath in sharply and stared at him for a brief moment before remembering that she was on stage and all the audience had their eyes on her. She took another little bow and politely scooped up each and every flower which was thrown onto the stage for her. With an armload of roses, gerberas, and carnations, she took another shy little bow before hurrying off stage, not looking for her father's face again.

∽

Anna hurried into the dressing room backstage that was kept just for her and Maisie. She knew she'd be alone for a while, for Maisie was the next act, and she could already hear the *oohs* and *ahhs* of the crowd as Maisie performed her wonderful acrobatics.

Anna sat down at her dressing table and took a few deep, steadying breaths. Had it really been her father in the audience, or was her mind playing tricks on her? Perhaps it was a man who looked like him just enough that she might be fooled in the semi-darkness of the music hall.

However, when the door was knocked on and abruptly opened, Anna was disabused of her comforting delusion. Her father walked in, closed the door behind him, and stood a few feet from her with his hands thrust into his pockets.

"You were wonderful out there, my sweet. No wonder they call you the Nightingale of Kennington," her father said, smiling at her, unsettling her. He'd hardly looked at her when they shared their miserable existence on the road, now he was smiling for all he was worth.

"Funny, really, given that I have no talent," Anna said, getting to her feet also, feeling so many emotions all at once, the overriding one being anger. "Don't you remember, Father? That's why you didn't bother to train me for anything in the circus; you could tell by looking at me that I had no talent."

"Now, that's not true, you know that I…"

"It was one of the last things you said to me before you abandoned me."

"Now, I didn't abandon you, I told you I'd be back, didn't I?"

"I don't believe for a minute that you're back because you want to be. If things had worked out for you in America, you'd have stayed there. You walked away, and you didn't care what happened to me. Well, I can tell you what you missed, if you like," she said, hands on hips, wondering how on earth he'd made his way backstage to her dressing room without being stopped. "The man you gave me to, yes, *gave me to*, tried to beat me, and then had me cast out onto the streets. But of course, you knew he might, didn't you? After all, I think you are perfectly well aware that he had beaten Lucy Lawrence and probably more people than that in the time you knew him. It didn't bother you though, did it? You left me there anyway."

"Now, I wouldn't have…"

"But that's how things work in the circus, isn't it? That's how things work in your world. Well, your world isn't my world anymore," she said, so furious that her fists were clenched at her sides.

"Think yourself so fancy, do you?" He looked shocked, and Anna knew why; he'd never heard his daughter say anything to him that wasn't connected to her care of him, his meals, his clothes, his every comfort. Now, here she was telling him exactly what she thought, no wonder it had come as such a great shock.

"Not fancy, just free."

"Look, you've done all right for yourself here, I'll give you that, but it's time to come home."

"Home? When did I ever have a home? This is the only home I've ever had," she said and spread her arms wide to indicate the entire music hall.

"I've managed to get us both back in with Gerrity, we start back with him in a few days. And we're going back to Lincoln, my sweet, just think of that! You liked Lincoln, didn't you?"

"What?" she said and shook her head violently. "I have just told you that Kelvin Gerrity tried to beat me and here you are telling me that I must go back to him?! Did you listen to a word I said?"

"I did, but you're my daughter, and you will do as you are told. Now, I know I left you and I don't doubt you're a little touchy about it, so I'll let this little outburst of yours go by the by this time. But understand this, Missy," he said, suddenly striding towards her and gripping her shoulders hard, shaking her, "you're still my daughter, my property. You're still my child."

"It's been three years since I set eyes on you, Father. I'm not a little girl anymore, I'm eighteen years old. Yes, that's right!" she said, her fear trying to overpower her anger and not entirely succeeding. "And you're right, I have made a good life for myself here. *Me*! I made it, not you. I don't owe you a single thing, and I am never, ever going back to the circus."

"You can sing, Anna. Mr Gerrity says that not only can you sing in the interval, but you might even have an act all of your own, a real place in the circus after all."

"I don't care what Mr Gerrity says."

"Then I'll make you care. Now, I've had enough of your lip, believe me." He was gripping her shoulders so hard now that she knew she would be bruised. "I'll give you the week to sort yourself out here, to give that fancy music hall man a bit of notice, and then I'll be back for you. I'll be back for you, and I will have Mr Gerrity with me, just in case you're thinking of putting up a fight. You're my daughter, you belong to me; that's the law of the land, and you very well know it!"

He let go of her suddenly, marching out of the room, leaving the door wide open.

Shaking and with the first sting of tears in her eyes, Anna dropped down onto the dressing table stool and felt her new, blessed life slipping through her fingers. She had attained her dream, she had soared like Lucy had dreamt, and now she was crashing back down to earth in a ball of fire.

CHAPTER 12

"Anna, what is it? What's wrong?" Jonathan came looking for her some ten minutes later, finding her leaning on the dressing table, her head in her hands as she sobbed.

"Oh, Mr Warner, I don't really know where to begin," she said, her throat tight and the reality of her situation truly dawning on her. She really was her father's property, even though he had discarded that property and not cared what happened when he went to America. Of course, these sorts of responsibilities only ever went one way, Anna knew that.

"That man really was your father? I didn't know whether to let him in or not, but he seemed so pleasant, so polite. Forgive me, should I have kept him away?" He looked so apologetic when she turned to stare at him; so, it had been Mr Warner himself who had let her father backstage.

"Yes, he really is my father. Oh, yes, he does seem polite, doesn't he? There are two sides to Bernard Bailey, Mr Warner. There is a nice, polite side that you and countless young women up and down the country are treated to, and then there is the ugly, selfish brute who left his fifteen almost sixteen-year-old daughter alone when he had a better offer in America."

"He just left you?" Jonathan looked dumbfounded.

"He left me with Mr Gerrity, and he left me knowing exactly what sort of man Mr Gerrity is. He didn't care what happened to me, but now he comes back to England, having failed in America, and tells me that I am his property and I am to go back with him to *Gerrity's Unbelievable Show*."

"He can't do that!" Jonathan said, taking a small wooden chair from the side of the room and carrying it across to where she was, sitting down in front of her.

"I'm still his daughter, Mr Warner, he can do what he likes; it's his right. And if you can believe it, now he admits I have some sort of talent. He must've discussed it with Mr Gerrity, and he tells me that Mr Gerrity will now let me sing in the interval, even as an act of my own," she said and shook her head, riddled with despair.

"So, they found out what a success you are in London, and the two of them are hoping to cash in on it," Jonathan said, his pale blue eyes narrowed to slits. "How…" Jonathan's kind soul couldn't seem to find the word.

"Despicable, sir, it's despicable. Because you know they will not pay me, not like you do. And it's not only that, but I can't bear to leave this place. You might think me silly, but this is the only real home I've ever known. I mean, I know it's not a home with a real family, but everybody here has begun to feel that way to me. Maisie, all the others, I couldn't bear to leave them," she said, knowing that it was Jonathan she couldn't bear to leave more than anyone.

"And I can't let you go, Anna. It's not the money, I have more than enough of that. It was my dream to have this place packed, and you've done that for me, you made that happen. This music hall comes alive when you sing, just your presence here…" he said trailed off.

"He's coming back for me at the end of the week," Anna said dolefully. "And he's bringing Mr Gerrity with him, just in case I think of putting up a fight."

"That a man could treat his only daughter that way," Jonathan said, shaking his head. "Well, I have an idea. You might not like it, but just hear me out." He looked suddenly apprehensive, nervous.

"Go on," Anna said, thinking that she would do just about anything to stay in Kennington.

"I could marry you. If I was married to you, then your father would no longer have any claim over you by law. He could never make you leave here; he could never make you do anything. You'd never have to set eyes on him again if that was what you wanted."

"You would marry me?" Anna said, her mouth falling open as she stared at him.

He looked so handsome, those pale blue eyes and that dark hair. He looked so fine in the black suit and tails he wore every night at the show. This might have been a dream come true, if only he loved her.

"If you want to, of course," he said, looking down at his hands for a moment. "I mean, it would be in name only. I'm not like Kelvin Gerrity or any other man who has treated you so badly, Anna. I wouldn't expect anything of you, I just want to keep you safe. I couldn't bear the thought of you going back to that life, being treated so badly and having your talent wasted on crowds of fools who only want to see poor desperate people suffering the worst imaginable deformities. How could a crowd like that ever appreciate the beauty of your voice?"

"Oh, Mr Warner…"

"Jonathan," he said finally and looked at her again, his face still full of apprehension.

"Jonathan, I can't marry you."

"It's all right, I understand," he said, his kindness shining through even now.

"No, I don't think you do understand," she said and decided to have the courage to explain it to him properly. "The thing is, I can hardly believe the kindness you've shown me ever since we first met. And now this, you offering to marry me just to save me from my father. I don't have the words to thank you properly for that, I really don't. But you don't love me, Jonathan, not as I love you. I love you so much that I couldn't bear to stop you from having a proper life, a real life, with another woman you could really love."

"Oh!" Jonathan said, all the tension suddenly disappearing from his face to be replaced with a broad smile. "Anna, how could you think I don't love you?" He began to laugh.

"You mean, you do? You do love me?" Anna asked, feeling suddenly breathless and a little dizzy. "But I thought… I mean, you kissed me once and you regretted it so terribly that… I thought you didn't like me."

"Anna, how could you think that? I did regret it, it's true, but not because I didn't like you. I regretted it because I had kissed you so suddenly, I hadn't given you any warning, nor any chance to turn me away. I had behaved just as so many other men have behaved in the past, and I was deeply ashamed of myself."

"You were nothing like any of the dreadful men I've known, Jonathan. You are a gentleman, not just in status, but right down to your very bones. I never thought anything else, not even when you kissed me."

"Then I'm starting to wish I had kissed you again because I've hardly been able to think of anything else for an entire year," he said and laughed heartily, the sort of laugh a man might give when he is suddenly relieved of a great emotional burden. "Anna, I think I fell in love with you the first time I heard you sing. That day when you were feeding the tigers at the circus, I heard your voice drift out through the canvas and I knew I had to find you. You have no idea how long it took me to find the slit in the tent to make my entrance, I must've walked around the thing three times before I did!"

He grinned and shrugged, and Anna laughed; could this really be happening? Did he really love her just as she had feared he never would?

"Are you sure, Jonathan? I mean, this is for life, isn't it? Are you sure it's me you want to be with?"

He rose to his feet without speaking and reached for her hands. He gently pulled her to standing and wrapped his arms around her. She felt warm and protected there, her head on his shoulder.

"Never doubt that I love you, Anna. I see right into your heart every time you sing, and I want nothing more than to have that heart as my own for the rest of my life. If you'll have me, it will make me the happiest man alive."

"Of course, I will," Anna said and felt the first tears of emotion. "I love you, Jonathan."

"And I love you, Anna," he said, and finally, he kissed her.

Anna felt complete. His lips were warm and smooth, and his kiss so much more passionate than that first tentative kiss had been. This was right, and she knew it; she could feel it deep in her soul. This was her dream. This was the plan God had for her.

EPILOGUE

Anna walked to the music hall, determined to spend the day practising. It had been a while since she'd sung in front of an audience, and she wanted to make sure that she would be as familiar with everything on stage as she had once been.

Jonathan would already be inside, setting off early as he did every single day, giving the music hall every ounce of his effort, just as he had always done. Anna admired him more and more with every day that passed, and she knew she would admire him more and more into the future.

Hurriedly crossing the street to the hall, Anna could see a small gathering of people standing around the latest billboard. Their attention was fully drawn by it, and she could hear them chattering among themselves.

"It will be quite something to see her back and no mistake!" one of the men said, nodding fiercely.

"It will that, it will that," a woman in the crowd agreed, and the others murmured affirmative.

Anna could see herself on the billboard, a brand-new photo taken just a few weeks ago. She was wearing a beautiful gown, pink, although its colour couldn't be seen on the black and white billboard poster. She stood behind them, reading the poster to herself.

"*The Nightingale of Kennington Returns!*" the poster proclaimed in bold black type. "*The unmistakeable Anna Bailey will be back for the summer season! Get your tickets now!*"

Anna smiled; she was looking forward to this. It had been four years now since she'd been a regular part of the show, although they had been four wonderful years.

Jonathan had married her that very week, the two of them departing the following morning on a steam train bound for Gretna Green in Scotland. He wasn't going to take any chances with the woman he loved; he wasn't going to give her rotten father an opportunity to drag her away from him.

All the performers had been thrilled; not only did they adore Anna, but they had the greatest love and respect for their employer also. They had quickly arranged the show so that it might go on without Anna, and one of the vaudeville comedy actors had enthusiastically agreed to take Jonathan's place as the show's compere.

The two young lovers had set off immediately, the wonderful journey to and from Scotland something that Anna knew she would never, ever forget.

She only ever saw her father once after that, almost two weeks after she had become a married woman. He'd arrived at the music hall furious with her, claiming her to be a devious little rat who had hidden from him and Mr Gerrity. There they had stood, her father and the hateful ringmaster, both of them so sure that they had every right to drag her away. That had been until her husband had stepped out of the shadows and told them otherwise.

The circus had moved on then, heading north as it always did after the tour of London finished. Bernard Bailey disappeared, taking up the reins of his old life, and she never saw hide nor hair of him ever again. She always looked out for billboards proclaiming *Gerrity's Unbelievable Show* was back in town, but they seemed to stay clear of South London, and Anna was grateful for that.

Before the little crowd had a chance to realise that the Nightingale of Kennington was right behind them, Billy Smith opened the side door of the music hall and beckoned her inside.

"Good morning, Billy," Anna said, her smile warm and bright as it always was when she saw her old friend. He was a young man now, almost fifteen years old.

"Good morning, Anna," he said; he'd never made any pretence, only ever calling her Anna, never Mrs Warner. He never even called her Miss Bailey, her stage name. They were friends, they always had been, they always would be. They had worked together in service, and Anna had never expected anything different. "Good job I saw you standing there before you got mobbed. They'll have been wanting their programme sheets signed, even their tickets! It's going to be a real crowd tonight, believe me! Folk have been coming in for tickets ever since that billboard went up. The Nightingale, eh?" he said and started to chuckle. "Mrs Bunker would be turned inside out by that one!"

"I just hope my voice is up to it, God willing." Anna said modestly.

"You know it is, Anna, don't be talking like that!" Billy chuckled as the two of them wandered into the hall.

"So, are you busy today?"

"I certainly am. I'm still introducing some of the acts, just as Mr Warner has trained me, but there's a chance of me getting on with the two vaudeville blokes. They need a young scamp like me, you see, to do a little bit of tumbling and rolling about and what have you."

"That's wonderful, Billy!" Anna said, so proud of him.

After her marriage, Anna had found herself unable to stop thinking about Billy. When she had realised that she was expecting her first child, thoughts of the little boy who had rescued her from the poverty of the street plagued her night and day. When she told Jonathan, he'd immediately sought out the little boy and offered him something better at the music hall if he had a mind to take it. Billy being Billy, had done a little bit of everything, making himself useful and talking ten to the dozen, having all the performers fall in love with him and his cheeky ways.

"It is, isn't it? Anyway, how are you getting on? How's that little Billy doing?" he said, grinning with pride as he always did when he spoke of Anna's baby son; his namesake, William Warner.

"Well, he's noisy and cheeky and adorable, so I suppose I picked his name just right, didn't I?" Anna said and ruffled his hair.

"And Lucy?"

"Lucy talks from the moment her eyes open until the moment they close at night. She is a lovely girl," Anna said, full of pride for her firstborn child, the child she had named after her dear friend. "Once I get my bearings again, once the rehearsals begin in earnest, I'll have them both come over, and you can see them for yourself."

"Now, won't that be a treat. Come on then, everybody is waiting for you," he said and held out his arm for her to take, leading her to the stage where the performers, her old friends, were eagerly awaiting her arrival.

The hall was packed to capacity when Anna Warner, or *Miss Anna Bailey* as she was still known to her adoring fans, took to the stage once more. A hush fell over them all as if they were already locked in a spell before she had even sung her first note.

It felt good to be back, even though she would only be performing two nights a week. She was a mother now, and even though the children had a nurse, still, she gave them every ounce of her attention. How different her life was, her fine home, her fine husband, her wonderful children. She could hardly believe she had started out her life living in that awful little wooden carriage with her father, travelling up and down the country with never a town to call their own.

Singing her first line, Anna felt as if she had never been away from the stage. She closed her eyes, imagining herself hanging out washing with her heart broken, and there she found the emotion that she always used to sing. It had never failed her before, and it certainly didn't fail now.

"*The boy I love is up in the gallery,*

The boy I love is looking now at me,

There he is, can't you see, waving his handkerchief,

As merry as a robin that sings on a tree..."

As she sang, she searched the audience for any sign of Jonathan, finding him in the front row looking up at her with rapt attention. She smiled at him, and she could hear her smile in her voice; how emotion made her sing even better!

When she finished, the audience rose to their feet immediately. They clapped and stamped their feet, and she could feel the vibration of it through the very wood of the stage. Her eyes filled with tears, but she blinked them back, not letting them fall. She bowed as the first of the flowers landed on the stage. There were so many of them, more than ever before, and the crowd was still clapping and cheering. After a few years away, Miss Anna Bailey, the Nightingale of Kennington, could still bring the house down.

She looked towards Jonathan and saw him get closer to the stage, a single red rose in his hand. He didn't throw it onto the stage, he held it up and she daintily crouched down at the very front of the stage to take it from him.

"I love you," he mouthed the words over the din of the appreciative audience, each and every one of them thoroughly enjoying so romantic a display.

"I love you too, Jonathan," she mouthed back, and finally, a little tear of pure joy made its way down her cheek.

THANK YOU FOR CHOOSING A PUREREAD BOOK!

We hope you enjoyed the story, and as a way to thank you for choosing PureRead we'd like to send you this free book, and other fun reader rewards...

Click here for your free copy of Whitechapel Waif
PureRead.com/victorian

Thanks again for reading.
See you soon!

OTHER BOOKS BY JESS WEIR

If you loved this story why not read other books by the same author?

The Midwife's Dream

The Mill Daughter's Courage

The Orphan Pickpocket's Christmas

LOVE VICTORIAN ROMANCE?

If you enjoyed this story why not continue straight away with other books in our PureRead Victorian Romance library?

Read them all...

Victorian Slum Girl's Dream

Poor Girl's Hope

The Lost Orphan of Cheapside

Born a Workhouse Baby

The Lowly Maid's Triumph

Poor Girl's Hope

The Victorian Millhouse Sisters

Dora's Workhouse Child

Saltwick River Orphan

Workhouse Girl and The Veiled Lady

OUR GIFT TO YOU

AS A WAY TO SAY THANK YOU WE WOULD LOVE TO SEND YOU THIS BEAUTIFUL STORY FREE OF CHARGE.

Click here for your free copy of Whitechapel Waif

PureRead.com/victorian

At PureRead we publish books you can trust. Great tales without smut or swearing, but with all of the mystery and romance you expect from a great story.

Be the first to know when we release new books, take part in our fun competitions, and get surprise free books in your inbox by signing up to our free VIP Reader list.

As a welcome gift you'll receive the story of the Whitechapel Waif straight to your inbox...

Click here for your free copy of Whitechapel Waif

PureRead.com/victorian

Printed in Great Britain
by Amazon